I0626248

The Blue Room

The Blue Room

VOL. 1

Kailin Gow

The Blue Room (The Blue Room Vol. 1)

The Blue Room (The Blue Room Vol I)
Published by Sparklesoup Inc.
http://www.sparklesoup.com
Copyright © 2014 Kailin Gow

For information, please contact:
Kailingowbooks(at)aol(dot)com.
First Edition.
Printed in the United States of America.

Kailin Gow

DEDICATION

To My Readers, Betas, and Kailin Krusaders, Thank You for All Your Love, Support, and Encouragement. You are truly one of the most important reasons why I'm blessed beyond measure.

Prologue

Terrence Blue

Some people, they're happy where they are, with what they have. Some people are happy with the little things in life – the feeling of sunshine on their faces, the sound of a baby's laugh, the taste of fresh-squeezed orange juice on their lips. They're happy with the music from the ice-cream truck down the street, with the sweet-looking girl who grew up next door and who doesn't ask too much, with the smell of fresh flowers growing on the edge of a cul-de-sac.

Not me.

See, there are things I don't go in for. And mediocrity is one of them. The way I see it, anybody who can get close enough to the best – close enough, I mean, to see it, smell it, taste it, almost bite it – and who doesn't is a sucker, through and through. Don't give me any of that BS about "mindfulness", about "being happy with what you have." I wouldn't buy it. The things I spend my money on are the things you couldn't even dream of affording. I spend my money on the best. The best women, the best booze, the best drugs. The best sounds. And there isn't a single person who's known me for longer than twenty minutes that's in any doubt of that.

So don't you think that anything less will satisfy me.

My name is Terrence Blue, and everybody knows I'm a hard man to please. I've poured thousand-dollar magnums of champagne down the drain. I've flushed fistfuls of cocaine down the toilet. I've thrown supermodels out of my bed because I don't like the color of their bras.

And I can afford to. So why shouldn't I?

Now, I'm a businessman, first and foremost. I'm no fool. I know that the money that comes in as a result of my reputation as a hard man to please more than makes up for the money I waste. It's a funny thing about this business, isn't it? The more money you burn, the

The Blue Room (The Blue Room Vol. 1)

more people keep throwing at you. I'm a magician. I make money disappear – then reappear. But everything's an illusion here in LA. Living out in La La land, you learn pretty quickly – or not at all. People want the illusion. They want to think they're in a night club like the Blue Room because they're better than all those other identical wannabes lining up outside the door. They wanna believe they're special. And with me, Terrence Blue, they feel special. And once you give them that feeling, they'll do anything to keep it going. You think coke is bad? Try that feeling. There's no more glorious, more addictive substance on earth.

That's all you need to know about me.

So here we are. Terrence Blue's Blue Room – equal parts Studio 54 and *Eyes Wide Shut*. A burlesque club where you can do more than look, if you know what I mean. My pride and joy. Where the girls can sing – but you'd be mesmerized even if you weren't looking at their voices.

Like this one girl. The girl singing now. The light's dark midnight blue on her face, but it only brings out that milky figure – her porcelain skin, that platinum blonde hair with little fingers waves in it like Jean

Kailin Gow

Harlow would have worn, there in a bikini bottom and bra encrusted with gems – gems from my private collection, I'll have you known – sapphires and rubies. And rubies at her lips, too – top shel makeup, studded with metallic dust, making those lips so bright and kissable you wouldn't mind stopping the song if it only meant you could pull that mouth onto yours. Her lashes so long – like they were trying to keep you away, like she had secrets to hide, that one.

    I knew her type. I go through dozens like her every day. Identical, like drones, robots, clones. Fresh from Kansas or Iowa or Idaho or wherever – big in church choir, dreaming of being a star, willing to do whatever it takes, scared of what that means. Lucky for her, though, she could sing. Staci Atussi had a voice that could knock your socks onto your hands, and she wasn't bad in a bikini either. Though she didn't want me mistaking her for one of *those* dancers, oh no, she was clear on that point. A prim little blush, pursed lips, *I'm not that kind of girl,* all of that. The way she blushed when she heard what patrons of the club regularly shelled out the big bucks to do with performers, you'd think she was a virgin or something.

The Blue Room (The Blue Room Vol. 1)

Maybe she was. You never know. Stranger things have happened in La La lands. But I can't say it's every day you get a virgin trying to claw her way to the top of the greasy pole at the Blue Room. I could have thrown her out, then and there. It's not good for business if the talent gets a reputation for being fresh with the high-rollers. People don't just come to The Blue Room to listen to a girl sing, after all. But I liked her. Something about her made me want to give her a second chance. Maybe she'd change her mind. I've been known to be convincing enough.

Not that I know too many virgins to convince. Let alone hot ones. The only one I could think of was Neve Knight, that hot little number who kept my brother wrapped around her finger. Either that, or Danny was keeping his success with her close to the chest. I figured the latter. The girl was hot, but from what I knew of my half-brother's reputation, he wouldn't be giving her a promise ring if he wasn't getting something. What a waste, I figured. A girl like that – with an emo brooder like my brother. I would have shown her a much better time. If she'd met me first – but them's the breaks, in La la land. It's all about who you know, and when. It's all about luck. And when it comes to chance, first one in always wins. Early bird and all that.

Besides, she was a nice kid, and I – many things that I am – am not. I go through women like breath mints. My idea of a long-term relationship is a weekend in Vegas.

But looking at Staci shake her hips, I start to wonder if maybe the whole virgin thing was just an act. As she starts unclasping her bra, letting those full and delicious breasts as loose as nature intended, I start to wonder if she's done this before. She knows what she's doing, that one. She knows what she's making us want – and she's making us believe that she wants it too. A real magic act. LA at its finest. She's moving across the stage all assured-like, like she knows exactly what's going on in every pair of trousers in the room.

But she's got another thing coming if she thinks she's got power over us. The kind of guys who I let into my club are the kind of guys used to getting what they want. They got in here, didn't they? And if one of them put down the right amount of cash, even the blushing Staci might find herself in one of those luxurious pleasure suites for the night, and then no doubt she could

The Blue Room (The Blue Room Vol. 1)

kiss her virginity goodbye.

Her breasts free, Staci starts wriggling out of her bottoms. I can see the contour of her hips. I can smell the desire in the room. The fierce wolf hunger. We're all feeling it.

Then, just as those delectable panties fall to the floor, something blocks my view.

"Danny!"

My half-brother, his chest so broad I can't see an inch of female flesh, is standing in front of me.

His finger is in my chest.

"Your office. Now."

Now, a man like me – we don't like to be rushed. We take our sweet time. But I don't mind saying in this case that – fully of my own free will, you understand – we went straight to Danny's office. You may have heard that Danny grabbed me by the shirt and dragged me there. I can't say. Had a bit to drink, after all.

"What do you want, big brother?" I almost spat in his face. "I was at the best part!"

"What were you thinking? What was going through your mind?"

"Well, just now I was thinking that those were

Kailin Gow

the nicest pair of..."

"I mean when you slept with her?"

Now, as I've told you, I'm not exactly a one-woman guy. *Her*, on any given week, could refer to between five and ten lovely ladies.

"You're gonna have to be more specific, bro."

"You gave her an alibi." Danny wasn't kidding around. He was the kind of man where cartoon smoke is a couple seconds away from blowing out your ears. "We can't prosecute her because of your alibi, and now she's gonna get away with it. Attempted murder."

I'm sure I could have listened to him, if I wanted to, but I'd had a bit to drink, and there was a gorgeous naked girl prancing around on the stage of the Blue Room, so I can't say I was paying a lot of attention.

"Attempted murder? What, man? I'm gone..."

"Attempted murder on Never Knight."

Now, I'm a lot of things, and I forget a *lot* of crazy nights, but I'm pretty sure that murder's not on my list of after-midnight vices.

"Bro, I would never. A walking bombshell like that – I would never do humanity the injustice of depriving her of one waking moment in our company."

- 11 -

The Blue Room (The Blue Room Vol. 1)

"You realize you're talking about my soon-to-be fiancee?" I'm sure a lot of people think Danny Blue is pretty imposing when he growls, but that's the thing about being someone's brother. You can't take them seriously when you've seen them soil their onesies after watching *Barney* that one time. "Anyway, your depravity, your lack of morals....to go so far as sleeping with..."

"Hey, I didn't sleep with Neve!" I had to admit it. It wasn't for lack of trying, but the girl really loved her boyfriend. And while I had to make a good show of wanting her – didn't want to offend her, after all – I respected that.

"Not Neve. Roni."

"Oh." Who hadn't slept with Roni? It was a rite of passage, like bar mitzvahs or your first beer.

"Don't you have any family loyalty? Don't you ever think with your brain, instead of with your..."

"I like to think I'm a creative thinker. Besides, I have the Blue family genes. Not like Dad didn't cuckold a bunch of sorry husbands in his day. May the best man score and all that."

"But *Roni.*" *I hate it* when my brother makes me

feel guilty. It's almost like he's morally superior or something. "It's like sleeping with the devil."

"But you beat me to that already, didn't you?" I played the cards I've got, and that card needed to be played.

"Before she got with Dad! And even then it was a mistake through and through." Danny mops the sweat from his brow. The man knows how to look brooding and serious even when he's screaming his lungs out. What a drama queen.

"It's not like I even knew she married our dad!" I feel I have a point. "She turns up at the club this one time – I mean, I can't keep track of who Dad marries. They all look the same, act the same, talk the same, walk the same. It's not like he asked us to the wedding. I don't do a background check on every girl I get with to see if Dad's also had her."

"You're disgusting. Don't you even bother getting to know a girl before..."

"Don't be so high and mighty with me! Before you were a lovesick puppy you were just as bad as me. Maybe worse."

"I've changed."

The Blue Room (The Blue Room Vol. 1)

Sure he has. Or better say *been changed.* By one Miss Neve Knight.

"Everything I do now is for love."

"Oh, go write that down in a song." I can't listen to this BS any longer.

"Already did." Danny's in my face now. "Just try and give me a reason to fire you, little brother. Just try."

Chapter 1

Terrence

I like it when Danny gets angry. Always did. To see that smug little face scrunch up in anger, to see those bright blue eyes blaze in the old Blue way. Someone like Danny Blue doesn't rage easy. Brooding, of course, but that's whole 'nother thing entirely. Danny Blue could brood for days and wouldn't get a single rise out of me. It's what he does, normally. Locks it all up inside. All that rage, all that heartbreak, all that feeling. Even when I deserve a good kick in the jollies, Danny Blue doesn't oblige. He just clenches up his heart like a fist. But that's Danny for you. Never wanting to give anyone else the satisfaction of seeing Danny Blue lose control. But not this time. That much, at least, I'm certain of. Danny's coming close – *this close* – to losing it all. His mind, his heart, his temper. And I'm enjoying the heck out of it.

All my life, Danny's been the good boy. The favored son. The one born to the only woman Clarence

The Blue Room (The Blue Room Vol. 1)

Blue ever really loved. Not like my mother. That good-for-nothing trash whore – that's how Daddy dearest used to refer to her. A pin-up model who had the audacity to age out of my dad's preferred age bracket, just when he moved up a tax bracket or two. How dare she, right? And my daddy never forgave her for it, nor for the millions she took with her when she finally upped and left one morning over the morning papers. We all saw the front page headlines: Clarence Blue – spotted with starlet. But that was many moons ago – and many wives ago.

Not that it mattered when it came to Danny and me. Our relationship was always that of the Cain and the Abel, the beloved and the despised. Clarence may have pretended to be disappointed in Danny Boy, may have pretended he couldn't stand the sight of that dark rosebud mouth of his – his mother's mouth – but deep down he loved the boy, loved him like he loved the woman he'd lost, like he loved his own flesh. Danny Blue was sired by the man my father was once, once upon a time. The man that knew how to love. The rest of us – we were all bastards. Illegitimate children. Sure, we were Clarence Blue's kids – at least the DNA tests said so, when they came back – and you've got another thing coming if Clarence Blue didn't insist on a DNA test for every potential progeny that came out of every starlet's belly – but not in reality. None of us were born to the Clarence Blue back when he was a real person, a person in love, a real man: not an ice-cold statue, a shadow of his former self. Luckily, most of us – I assumed – were born to cocktail waitresses, strippers, people who wouldn't make a fuss. Not one of his wives – or concubines, I should say. Just me. But that didn't make me Clarence Blue's *legitimate* son. I certainly wasn't the son he wanted. The flesh of his flesh. The bone of his bone. And so my father never loved me.

But Danny – oh, boy, that's another story. Danny was the apple of my father's eye. But for all that, he didn't have what it took. The Blues Empire was handed to him on a silver bloody platter – but Danny was too squeaky-clean to grease the wheel. He's an innocent, you see. Likes to eat oysters and drink champagne, but doesn't want to know how the sausage gets made. Doesn't know that the big business comes not from our shiny luxury hotels or the deals made in the boardroom over skyscrapers and nightclubs, but here. In the

The Blue Room (The Blue Room Vol. 1)

bedroom. Reeking, filthy, smelling of sex. Here, where the businessmen make the real deals – over the naked buttocks of a stripper, dusted with blow. Here, where you could get blackmailed into signing away your fortune to my father – just by being caught with the wrong lips thrusting against your groin. Here, where desire made you lose your mind, your marbles, your millions. I knew how the game worked. And I knew how to play it. Fortunes aren't made on oil or steel. They're made on flesh. All the oil in the world can't make up for the scent of a woman's sweat.

Danny never understood a word of that. He always held himself as so much better than the rest of us, so much purer, so much more deserving of affection and love. But when he's got the rage in his eyes and the rumbling of thunder, that blazing in his belly – then you know the truth. He's no better than I am. Not a single solitary fucking whit. I guess that's why I love making him as angry as I do. I guess that's why I love goading him on. Because it's proof: hard, solid, eye-bulging proof, that Danny Blue is no better than I am. No more deserving. And if Daddy Dearest loves him more, that's nobody's fault but his own. That's the sickening chance in the universe. That you can be loved so much – and not even deserve it.

Everyone loves Danny, after all. Like Neve. That sweet little number. It's not just that she's pretty – you can get a dozen dimes for a dime a dozen, if you know what I'm saying – this is Hollywood, after all. She's got something else. Some inner strength. A sharpness. I think if you showed her this business, let her get her hands dirty, she'd run it well. She knows what it takes to survive in this town. Which really means: to thrive, because only the lion, the tiger, the king of the jungle is the winner. Everyone else, even just half-a-rung lower on the ladder to success, is a loser. And you know what that means, don't you? They get eaten alive.

Now, Roni. That was a different story. Roni wasn't just about the sex to me. It's true, when I first met her, I didn't know she was my father's latest slam piece. But I'll be honest with you for a second. It wouldn't have made a grain of sand's worth of difference if I had. In fact, once I found out, it made it all the sweeter to have her squealing and moaning in my bed. It meant I had something that my father didn't. I had something he couldn't have. After years of underestimating me, of

The Blue Room (The Blue Room Vol. 1)

telling me I was worthless, of telling me I'd never measure up, my father had finally lost the one thing to me he thought he could never lose: a woman's touch. Screwing Roni was like sticking it to my father, once and for all.

At least, it was. Until I found out about her and Danny. Found out she had a thing for Blues men: that she wanted to create a matched set. Get all three of us inside her. And maybe I wouldn't have minded so much if I hadn't cottoned on that she loved the bastard. Really loved him, in as sick and twisted a way as a girl like Roni was capable of loving. And that's what got me. Right between the ribs – slice-like. That even Roni, who couldn't love anyone, could love him. More than me.

I'm not going to say I hated my brother. I loved him – in my way. I just wish he could fall on his stupid face once in a while, you know? And you wouldn't feel any different – if you were me. In fact, you'd feel exactly the bloody same.

"I'm trying," I say to him. "Believe me." Like I had to convince him not to fire me. Like I had to grovel. "I'm bringing in new acts all the time. Look at that girl up there. Singer, stripper, whatever. She's riling up all the patrons. She's just what we need, here. Someone fresh. Someone virginal."

Danny looks disgusted. Still had that self-righteous little smirk on his face. "Honestly, I don't know why we still have this place. Just because it's dear old dad's pet project..."

"Pet project?" Danny didn't understand a thing.

"It's twisted, Terrence."

"It may be twisted, but it's brilliant. A private club so elite its membership registrar might as well be the Who's Who of the world. Who knew so many of the world's most influential people were also the kinkiest, the most depraved, the most...well, I guess maybe you'd assume so, wouldn't you?"

"But just because we have to manage this place, Terrence..."

"What?"

"It doesn't mean we have to be like them! It's all fantasy here. But it's like a drug. You become addicted to it – but at the same time, Terrence, it'll pull you in so deep. You can't afford to get addicted to it. The sex, the smell, the feeling – it will take over everything you do. Especially since you're around it all the time. I'm worried

The Blue Room (The Blue Room Vol. 1)

about you, Terrence. The patrons, they only come here once in a while, to play-act at living this life. But you, Terrence. You're *in* it. You're in it bad and you're in it deep. And whatever sick, disgusting fantasy you're acting out with Roni – you need to quit it, now."

"Why?"

Danny pretends not to hear me. "And that girl on stage --"

"Yeah, the *virgin*." I like the sound of the words on my tongue.

"Virgin or not, Terrence, you'd better take care of her. Make sure she doesn't get abused by some of the rougher patrons around here. She's not a pro – she doesn't know what she's doing. She doesn't even know what kind of a place this is, does she?"

"It's Hollywood. *Every* kind of place is this kind of place."

"You don't know that."

"I bet she does."

"They'll eat her alive, Terrence. And this place – it'll eat you alive, too."

I can't believe my ears. I remember back when Danny was worse than me, when he slept with more girls, took more drugs, did more everything. I remember when he was so deep in the hole it was me who had to drive him home, me who had to pour cold water on his face, give the girls some hundreds in an unmarked brown envelope and send them home with a promise on their lips never to tell another living soul what they had seen him do.

"I just want to go home." Danny's brow is covered in sweat. "I just want to get back home to my girlfriend, sit on the couch, watch some TV, relax. Be with the woman I love. Get away from this place, from this sickening atmosphere. I don't want any part of this." He sighs so heavily. "So everything we talked about. You clear?"

"Good and clear." My voice is clipped, a mockery of professionalism. The way I bet he thinks his sounds.

"Now, I'm heading home."

"But..." I can't stop myself. "Don't you want to hear whom I've booked for next week's performance?"

"Whatever it is," Danny doesn't even stop to look at me. "It had better be good."

I can't resist a grin. Here it is. My ace in the

The Blue Room (The Blue Room Vol. 1)

hole. "Oh, it is. It definitely is. Even you would approve."

"Uh-huh..." Danny turns to go.

"The Never Knights. Next weekend."

Danny's mouth opens wide with shock. I love how it looks. "How? What? Why?"

"Ask her yourself."

That's all I say as I close the door in his face.

Chapter 2

Unfortunately, my victory doesn't last for particularly long. No sooner have I taken in the joyous sight of my brother's shocked face, his mouth agape, gaping like a goldfish that had been lifted into the air, then a knock sounds at the door.

I figure it was Danny, desperate for information. I figured his plan was to humble himself if he had to, if it meant figuring out what Neve Knight was doing at the Blue Room. A perfect plan, if I do say so myself. Getting Danny's dime onstage for all our patrons. Having her shake those delectable hips of hers in front of all those men who think they can have her. Now, when I say Neve agreed, I'm being almost completely truthful. Neve agreed to a gig. A gig at a "burlesque club." Girls all love burlesque these days. It's almost trendy. Didn't quite tell her the full extent of her duties, or how much she'd be expected to take off in the process. But she'd

The Blue Room (The Blue Room Vol. 1)

figure all that out in good time. And Neve's a swell girl, I reckon. A real star. The kind of girl who will do what it takes to get the audience growling. Even if it means throwing off her shirt, her bra, her underwear – but now I'm getting distracted. What I mean is, a girl like her – she's no prude. Loyal to Danny or not, she's got some spice in her. That much I can see, even from miles off. It was a real pleasure having her sign on the dotted line. The Never Knights: onstage at the Blue Room.

Even Daddy would have been proud at my daring. I couldn't help but grin to myself, thinking all the while: *now that's how you handle a girl.*

So when the knock sounds, I figure it's Danny. He's going to beg me to reconsider, to axe the gig, to nix Neve and all her Knights of the Round Table once and for all. He doesn't want to see the girl he loves shaking her money-maker in the faces of the world's greatest money-makers. He doesn't want her to get seduced by a fat wad of hundreds waved into her face by men who could blow their nose with that kind of money and not even blink one of their billion-dollar eyelashes.

But it's not Danny at all. I mean, Danny's there, but he's skulking in a corner, looking annoyed. Like he doesn't want to see me again for at least a hundred years. But he has to, because Troy Baker, our head of security, is standing in the doorway, with the kind of frightened-rabbit expression on his face that men as big and strong and brawny as he is only get when faced with someone even more powerful. In this case, me.

"Sorry to interrupt." The man's always deferential. Not a good look on a man of his girth. "My apologies, Mr. Blue."

"Go on," I say, as lightly and airily as I can manage it. "What's the matter, Troy?"

"There's, uh," Troy coughs and looks like he'd rather be anywhere else but here. "There's been an incident."

He flinches, and already I know the news isn't good. I'm not one to shoot the messenger, but my father was, and Troy doesn't yet know I'm a heck of a better man than my father ever could be.

"The new girl, Staci." Troy's eyes are on his shoes. "When she finished with her performance, just a couple minutes ago, she was walking off to get cleaned up when one of our, *ah*, patrons came over to her. Apparently he wanted a little *tete a tete* in his hotel room. Ideally lasting till morning."

Danny rolls his eyes.

"Come on?" I shrug. "What's the big deal? Happens all the time."

"The lady wasn't having it," Troy tries to be as delicate as possible. "She told him she'd rather spend her time elsewhere."

A rock drops in my stomach. None of my girls *ever* tells a patron she'd rather spend her time anywhere else than in his bed.

"He got upset?" I start thinking up damage control, concocting the numbers of girls I know would be happy to replace the skittish Staci in a heartbeat. Maybe two at once would assuage his hurt feelings...

"Worse." Troy's not having any fun at all. "He got persistent."

"Yeah?" I'm not liking the sound of this. I'm not liking the sound of this at all.

"She kept on refusing."

"Good for her." Danny's voice is sharp as steel. "Glad someone in this joint has got some principles."

"He got handsy."

"I'm not calling the cops, Troy..."

"*She* got handsy."

Now I'm getting it. It dawns on me, and the feeling is sickening. "Oh, no, Troy. She didn't..."

"Right in the balls, sir."

Instinctively, I wince and look down at my groin.

"Oh, *damn*."

"It gets worse, sir." Troy's staring at the door like it's a naked coed covered in strawberry ice cream.

"Don't tell me."

"He fell back. Hit his head on the table. He's out cold."

"*Shit*."

"Serves him right," Danny growls under his breath, but I ignore him.

"We'd better go deal with this, then." Danny and I follow Troy out to the main room of the club, and I find myself wondering about the effects of a concussion on short-term memory. If it's mild amnesia, I think, maybe he'll forget the number one rule of the Blue Room: that there are no rules, especially when it comes to the girls on stage.

A crowd's already formed. I sighed a temporary

The Blue Room (The Blue Room Vol. 1)

sigh of relief for our no-cell-phones policy. At least I can be reasonably certain the paps aren't getting hold of this as we speak. The balding, wiry man with a furious red welt on his forehead is Angus Martin, one of the head honchos at Walton & Brothers, the biggest hedge fund on this or any other continent. Not the kind of man you like to piss off. I gulp.

Danny looks at me, his eyebrows arched. "Your policy, brother. Your problem."

"It's gonna be okay!" I pretend like I'm cool with what's happening. Like it's all part of the plan. We get Troy to lift the man up. "He's going to the Empire Suite at the Blue Hotel." I whisper in Troy's ear. "Call Brandi and Bunny. Tell them to wear their skimpiest satins and to be there when he wakes up, right in the middle of them. He'll think he hit his head on the headboard in a moment of, ah, ecstasy."

Troy nods and lifts up Angus, fireman-style.

When we're alone, Danny grabs me by the shoulder, pushing me up against the wall. He's got that gravelly, growly Tom Waits-style voice he puts on when he's really, really angry. And for the first time, it hits me. Danny Blue isn't playing around.

Kailin Gow

"That girl's probably sobbing her eyes out in the dressing room," he hisses.

"She'd better be." I try and smooth my lapels. "After all, she's out of a job."

"How could you hire a girl like that?"

"Like what?"

"Like she doesn't know what she's getting into. A non-pro."

"Everyone's a pro if the price is right." That's what my father always said. "And that's what the clientele like best. The virgins who go wild. Not pros."

"It's a different crowd, Terrence. You know that. She knows that. The girl can sing – but this isn't a place for singers. It's not a place for Never Knight, either. It's a different world at the Club than it is out there. If you mix them, someone's going to get hurt. And if it's Neve, then I swear, Terrence, I am going to come after you so hard..."

I grit my teeth. How *dare* Danny be so self-righteous, after all the shit he used to pull? "That girl knew what she was getting into." Didn't she? "She begged me to give her a chance to start here. That she could take care of herself. 'I want to make it as a star.'

The Blue Room (The Blue Room Vol. 1)

That's what she said."

Danny looks like he's about to heave into my face. "She looks barely legal, if you ask me. I hope to heaven you checked her ID."

"I did."

"Some sick bastards here would like it if she weren't even out of high school. But do you realize what trouble we could get in...."

"Relax, bro. She's twenty-one. Older than *your* piece of jailbait..."

"Don't...call...her...that." Danny's eyes are practically bulging out of his skull. I love ribbing this guy, I swear. Making him mad is more fun than an amusement park in July. He deserves every ounce of irritation he gets, after all. Danny grew up a Blue, all of the perks, everything he wanted out of life handed to him on a shiny silver platter, spoon in the mouth and all. He needs someone to rub his nose in the dirt a little, from time to time. Keeps him sane. Keeps him good.

"It's not the same." Danny grimaces. "Neve's used to this world. She grew up in it. Being Keith Knight's daughter – she practically had vodka in her nursing bottle. She's used to fending off guys like these losers. But Staci – twenty-one or not, she's had a much more sheltered life."

I roll my eyes. "Growing up in Vegas, you mean?"

"Not everywhere in Vegas is like the strip, Terrence."

"She's got an idea of what the club is about."

"As long as Angus doesn't sue..."

"He won't." I'm confident Bunny and Brandi will see to that.

"And make sure the clientele know the rules. No means no. Even when you're a multibillionaire. And I refuse to have it any other way."

"Harsh."

"Revoke his membership if you have to. I'm not founding a business empire based on rape!"

"The girls know what..."

"No means no, Terrence." Danny's so passionate it's almost terrifying. "Whether she's out on the street or working the Blue Room. Our girls have a choice. They always have a choice. You got that?" His look is menacing. "Got that?"

He lets me up. My back is killing me.

The Blue Room (The Blue Room Vol. 1)

"Got it."

Danny Blue, in the right, as usual. Just my luck.

"And that goes double for you. You can't sleep with any of the girls here. Even if they consent. You're in a position of power over them – you can't abuse that."

"Like I'd need to use my position of power to get some tail. I can get plenty of that on my own. And I'm not so inclined at the moment. Roni's keeping me busy."

"Just because you're a Blue doesn't mean you have to act like our father," Danny scoffs. "You can keep it in your pants for a change."

"But fucking all and sundry is a family tradition." I grin at him, but he isn't having it.

"Not anymore." Danny looks grim. "I'm the head of the Blues now."

Chapter 3

Staci

I'm in my dressing room, trying my best not to cry. It's not working. My tears are snaking through the glitter on my face, leaving ugly mascara trails of blue and purple all down my made-up cheeks.

This, I think to myself. *This is how stars die.* For a second, it was like a dream. A fairytale. A Hollywood success story. Everything I ever wanted. I was on that stage, singing my heart out. The men in the audience – I recognized some of them. Big shot producers, directors, studio execs. The kind of guys who could make a girl's career.

And I was so stupid. So bloody stupid. I thought I could get in on talent. That singing like a nightingale was the way to impress them, to make them take my

The Blue Room (The Blue Room Vol. 1)

name and number, to make them think of me when it came round to casting time. But I was a fool, through and through. I had faith, stupid, naïve, blind faith, in the power of my voice.

All anyone wants in Hollywood is the power of the tits.

I felt anger swelling with my breast. The kind of rage it's tough to withstand at the best of times. But right now, I was livid. It felt like everything I'd ever wanted, everything I'd dreamed of – it had been so close. I smelled it. I tasted it. I breathed it all in. Fame. Fortune. Success. E: True Hollywood Story, right at the beginning. The moment where everything changes. That lucky break. I inhaled it like oxygen.

And then there it was. Gone. Empty air. Shattered glass. The shards of broken dreams all around me.

Maybe I should have gone with Angus Bolton. Maybe I should have done what he asked. It's only sex, right? Only flesh. What's flesh, transient, mortal, when you can have fame: which lasts forever? I'd have been getting the better end of the bargain, right? That's what I'm thinking, right now. That's what I'm thinking, with the tears streaming down my face, trying so hard to make sure nobody hears me cry.

To make sure Terrence Blue doesn't hear me cry.

He's the worst of all. He knew – this whole time, I feel sure. He *knew* what I'd be asked to do. Maybe he thought that I'd give in. That I'd succumb with the flashbulbs in my face and money waved at my tits. Maybe he thought I had desires I didn't even know I had until everyone's drunk and sweaty and the need is pouring off all our backs.

He's wrong. He's wrong about me, I tell myself. I'm not that kind of girl. I'm not his kind of girl. I don't even like him. Sure – when I first met him, sitting across from him in that swivel armchair in his private office – I felt a certain something. Not even attraction. Just, like, a heating of the blood. A prickle down my spine. But Terrence Blue is a pro – no less than the girls he hires. He knows how to sell sex. It's positively written in his DNA. Being attracted to Terrence Blue is like admiring a Michelangelo sculpture. It's just what you do. It doesn't mean anything. Maybe some other girl would find him sexy, with his cocksure smile and that swivel of his hips like he could just thrust any girl against the wall at a

The Blue Room (The Blue Room Vol. 1)

moment's notice, and she'd moan with ecstasy because of how lucky she is to have him. Maybe that's how it works, for other girls. Not for me.

I don't care about his eyes, those shining, piercing blue eyes that get right under your skin. I don't care about his silky soft hair, black, to his shoulders, lustrous. I don't care about his face, chiseled to perfection, but with a few flaws that indicate mischief, nor harmony or his full sinful lips like a rock star's lips.

"Staci?"

I don't care about his voice, either. Not when it's low and dark like this. Like he's whispering into my ear, trying to make me wet.

"How are you? I just came to see how you're doing."

I wipe my tears away with the back of my hand. I'd melt into the floor if Terrence Blue saw me cry. I'm supposed to be worldly, street-smart, experienced. Used to the attentions of horny men. Not some inexperienced virgin recent college grad, desperate for a job but unable to cope with its demands. A girl who gets hysterical when a man puts his hand on her ass. I need to convince him that I can handle this. This job, this world. That I can sing my heart out, and shake my tits to boot.

Rita could handle it, after all. My old college roommate, Rita was a gorgeous girl with long dark hair and blue eyes almost as piercing as Terrence's. She'd funded med school on that stage. Sure, there had been odd times – times when she didn't come home at night, times when she vanished for weeks on end – but she'd always texted me. Just to say "I'm fine. Don't wait for me." And she'd always come back. The last time, she told me she'd met someone. A wealthy man, a handsome man. A patron at the club. Mr. X., she called him. He was too famous, apparently, for me to know who he really was. She wasn't sure if he loved her or he loved her cup size, but she was happy. Happy enough to give up med school and live on his largesse. She left college and the last I heard, she was wearing Cartier. I figure she was happy. She wasn't broke, at least. And right now, not-broke was all I could focus on.

Well, that, and Rita.

One Facebook Message from her. "I'm in too deep. And I don't know how to get out." Sent from the Grand Blue Towers, a luxury hotel where the Blue Girls were frequently put up for the night. She never answered

The Blue Room (The Blue Room Vol. 1)

my calls. She never answered my emails.

I was going to find out what happened to her.

"Staci?"

Did Terrence use this voice on Rita, I wondered? That smooth voice, so husky with need. I knew I couldn't trust him. But when I felt my nipples harden, involuntarily, I knew his voice had the desired effect.

"What do you want?" My voice was soft. I couldn't stand to look up into his eyes.

His fingers on my bare shoulders seemed to burn into my skin. I could feel him tightening his grip on me. "Man...I was so turned on watching you on stage just now, Staci. I've seen a lot of girls at this club. And not one of them has a delectable pair of tits like yours. I just want to take them in my hands..."

I didn't move. I let him touch my breasts. I froze.

"I want to take them in my mouth..."

"Is that part of my job description?" I jerked back. Got control over myself again. "Because I'm pretty sure that's illegal."

"Your job," Terrence leans in so close I can smell the musk on him, masculine, sensual, and delicious. "Is to create a fantasy. To make men's fantasies come true. And not just any men. Only the most prestigious, the most powerful of men come here, knowing how exquisite our tastes are in selecting women for the Blue Room. That's why we put you up in the nicest hotels, give you everything you could desire. Food, beauty treatments, etiquette training, pampering beyond belief..."

"So I can fuck whoever pays you?" Now I'm getting mad.

"You'll do what you're willing to do. Nobody is forcing you to sing."

"I came here to sing," I say, still barely believing Terrence's words.

"You did sing." Terrence leans in and, before I can jerk away, takes my lower lip into his mouth, sucking it gently. It tingles and I almost moan. "You taste just as good as I imagined."

I pull away. I'm not going to let him distract me, not for a second.

"You're expecting me to have sex with patrons if I want to keep your job."

He doesn't listen. He's pressing me up against the wall, kissing me passionately, his tongue flicking

The Blue Room (The Blue Room Vol. 1)

against mine until I moan again in spite of myself. I despise him, but somehow I don't push him away.

I have to stay calm. To keep my job. To find out what happened to Rita.

But it's hard to stay calm when a boy who looks like Terrence Blue is pressing his body against mine.

"You surprise me, Miss Atussi. From the look in your eyes, I thought you wanted something else entirely. You're more than you seem."

"What are you talking about?"

"You may act all sweet and innocent, Atussi, but when you're on stage, you're the sexiest woman alive. You want something. You have a hunger in you. And I want to find out what it is." He presses my hand to the hard-on in his pants. It's enormous. Bestial.

But I push him away.

"I want you to stay..." he groans.

I want to stay, too. But I won't let him take advantage of me that easily. I took a deep breath, forcing myself back into control.

"Another day," he says. "You get another chance. Understood?"

"I'm not going to whore myself out, Terrence," I

say.

I think I detect a hint of a smile. "Good," he says. "But if you change your mind – remember, wealthy and powerful men take very good care of themselves. They have the money to. And they often make wildly passionate lovers. Most women would love to be their mistresses, to be taken care of by them, to be fucked by them."

"Not me." I make it as clear as possible.

But still, somehow, I let him trace his fingers up my inner thigh. I let him rub his fingers against my panties, then slide them aside. I feel those gasping tremors of pleasure as his fingers gently and tantalizingly rubbed the most sensitive and heated part of me to the point where I clench down on my lower lips to keep from moaning loudly, but my voice deep from the center of my chest groaned softly, "Oh, Terrence."

His voice is husky with need.

"What if that patron was me?"

Chapter 4

My whole body is tingling. I've never felt like this before. The shiver running up and down my spine; the way my blood is boiling in my veins. The way my heart is ricocheting against my chest so hard that it feels like I'm being beaten up from the inside out. All of that is new to me – so new.

Sure, I've felt desire before. Or, at least, I think I have. I've kissed boys, and fumbled here and there, and from time to time explored the outskirts of that land of pleasure I've never visited, not really. I'm experienced enough, I suppose. Although – I think with a sigh – by the standards of the Blue Room I'm practically celibate. I'm certainly the only virgin here.

It's not that I have anything against sex. Sex is what brought me into the world, after all, the only good thing my father ever did for me. I never held out for any particular reason. Except maybe idealism. The idea that when I knew, I'd *know*. That this was the person I wanted to lose my virginity to. In my head it had been a romantic realization. All about love, about pretty pink clouds and princess ribbons, about rings and promises of undying devotion. I'd never dreamed that my body would respond to the touch of a man like this. I'd never dreamed that it would respond without any promises of romance all – and to the most repulsive man I'd ever met, a player, a huckster – and maybe more. Whatever happened to Rita, I have no doubt that Terrence, even if he's not behind it, knows what's going on. He knows where she is.

I have to remember that. I tell myself that much. I have to remember that, even when his hand is on my thigh, his fingertips tracing ever so slightly the contours of my knee, then sliding upwards toward my panties again, I have to remember that, even when his musk is filling my nostrils, driving me wild, driving me mad. I have to *stay calm. Stay cool. Stay in control.*

But I couldn't deny what my body wanted. Physically, all I wanted was for Terrence to have his way with me then and there. I wanted it so badly I felt I could taste the need. I'd never known that sure a desire existed,

The Blue Room (The Blue Room Vol. 1)

a desire so strong, so potent, like the hottest spice or the most intoxicating wine, to make everything else in the world seem so vague in comparison. I'd never known temptation like this.

But I wasn't about to lose my virginity to Terrence. I know what it's like, after all, to get knocked up to a man who doesn't deserve you. I've seen men like him before. Players. Men who don't care about women except as receptacles for their desire and need. Good-looking men who have it all – wealth, looks, power, and that mysterious brand of sociopathy that so often comes along when you've got all those things in one package.

Men like my father.

Norma Rae, that was my mother's name. Stage name, of course – she wanted it to be Norma Jean but her managers said that was too on the nose. She wanted to go Broadway, go Hollywood. Instead, she went to my father's bedroom. He saw her in the chorus line and wanted her then and there, just like Terrence wanted me, just like I wanted him. In a movie, this would have been her ticket to fame and fortune, real romance. In a movie, he would have lifted her out of poverty and ambition and made her a star.

Kailin Gow

But life isn't like the movies. Life isn't like Hollywood. In real life, the men who seduce you knock you up and abandon you, leave you without a penny – a penny they could well afford. Just because they can. I mean, my dad wouldn't even have had to talk to my mother again, just to make sure she was taken care of. Men like him have secretaries to do things like that, remembering important things like their wives' birthdays and how many illegitimate daughters they have. But my dad, he didn't even care enough to send along enough money to keep my mom's health insurance going.

Pregnancy destroyed my mother's body. She always pretended like it didn't – joked she ate too much – but beneath the smile, beneath her attempts to spare me the guilt I always felt for existing, I saw the truth. Hollywood chewed her up and spit her out. Nobody wanted a showgirl with stretch marks. She never got married, never even had a boyfriend. Worked five or six jobs at once. None of them enough to give her insurance. None of them enough to treat the cancer that now ravaged her body.

She's in hospice, now.

And my father? He's probably here tonight.

The Blue Room (The Blue Room Vol. 1)

Sitting in the crowd. Putting those hundreds down another girl's G-string.

A girl no older than my mother was twenty-two years ago.

I would never have come back here, to dance for men like him. Not if I didn't want to know what happened to Rita. Not if I didn't want to get my own back on the Blue Room, and places like it – places that ruined the lives of the people that I loved.

I clung to that, and it gave me strength. It gave me the strength not to give in, even as Terrence moved his fingers over my most intimate part, giving me so much pleasure that I couldn't help myself when I moaned his name.

So, this is what desire was like. Scorching desire. The kind that leaves nothing in its wake but ash.

"So..." His voice is in my ear, tickling my earlobe, making my throat close up and my heart race. "What do you say?"

"To what?" I already know what.

"Me taking caring of you. Making sure you're at your peak, in terms of health and beauty. And if you so choose, you'll get first pick of the many, many men who will want to pick you. Move into Blue Towers. Get a King-Sized bed, a jacuzzi – all the luxury a girl like you could want."

A girl like me. Like he knows me.

Like he knows what I want.

I want the truth. That's what I hope to find in Blue Towers.

"Will you be there?" I try to sound sassy, but it comes out a whisper.

"Do you want me to be?" He looks me up and down, his smile so sure, like he's already won.

I don't answer him. I don't trust myself to answer intelligently. I think my body will do the talking for me the second I open my mouth.

"I don't usually bother going into the Towers to visit the girls. Day to day maintenance isn't my style. It's not exactly my area. I don't mix business and pleasure unless I've got a very good reason to do so."

He moves his hand away and I want to scream.

"Are all the girls who work here staying at the Towers?" Meaning, *is Rita at the Towers now*?

"Most, not all. Some live with their families. Not a lot, as you can imagine..."

The Blue Room (The Blue Room Vol. 1)

"Do any – you know – go away with the patrons?" *Is that where Rita went? Is that why I haven't heard from her since that last message?*

"So many questions, Miss Atussi." He pulls away completely. My flesh is on fire. "Are you planning on going away already – when just a second ago you said you didn't want to go away with any of us?"

"No – no." I clarify quickly. "Why would I?"

He leans in and kisses me again. I don't know what game he's playing, but whatever it is, he's got the upper hand. I bristle at how easy it is for him. "Picture me as your patron. Your lover. Taking pleasure in giving you pleasure. Taking pleasure in tasting you." His kiss is so deep I can barely breathe.

I close my eyes. Despite myself, I let him part my lips. I let him put his hand back between my legs.

"People always think this business is about women giving men pleasure. But not me. What can I say. I guess I'm a feminist." I want to smack that grin off his face. Right after he finishes fingering me. "I think women should enjoy themselves just as much. Maybe more."

"I have no problem enjoying myself." I snap

back into sense. "Responsibly."

"Everyone here is safe, if that's what you're worried about. Members have to get an STD test before they get their card, regular check-ups thereafter. The girls, too."

He moves his lips down to my breasts. I inhale sharply as he takes one of my nipples in his mouth. "Does this feel dangerous to you?"

I can only sigh in response.

"I knew it." He smiles wickedly and I can't stand it; I let it happen anyway. "I knew it. I knew there was a bad girl in there somewhere. I saw it on stage. I saw the real you. Everyone saw her. And many people – they want to see her again. In a private room. Alone."

He moves his mouth to my other breast.

"You are intoxicating, Miss Atussi. So pure – yet there's a fire in you. I'm sure enough of that. Maybe you'll even make me break my personal rule. If you want me to. I'll show you how to unleash that fire. I'll make you crave pleasure. I'll make you need it. Wouldn't you like that? Wouldn't you like everything I could give you?"

I can't tell if he's playing me or I'm playing him.

The Blue Room (The Blue Room Vol. 1)

What he's offering me is access, plain and simple. Access to him. And with it, maybe, the Blue Room's secrets.

"Yes," I said. I don't know if I mean it.

"Then move into the Towers, Staci."

I want to moan again.

"It's time to live."

I nod. Slowly.

Even now, I don't know which of us is winning.

Chapter 5

My ears are ringing. The orgasm I've experienced is so violent, so earth-shaking, that the sky goes black and white above my eyes. I can't see a thing. I'm shaking, all over. My body is trembling like a twig in the depths of a thunderstorm. My skin is so sensitive; I can feel every inch of the satin sheets against my spine.

I look around me in shock. For a second, my hands clutch around empty air. My fingers trace nothingness.

Then...

Who was it that held me? Who was it that wrapped his legs around my waist, that thrust inside me, that let his chest clench against my chest, that let me feel his smooth skin, his taut muscles, his rippling strength?

I'm breathing shallow, hard, so loud I'm afraid I'll wake up the person in the room next to me. I'm breathing so hard I *can't* breathe.

The Blue Room (The Blue Room Vol. 1)

It was only a dream, Staci. I feel stupid, saying it out loud. But I have to, to reassure myself, to stop my heart from beating as fast as a hummingbird's. Whatever I felt, whatever pleasure I succumbed to in the night – it wasn't real. That face, those glittering blue eyes with that wicked smirk in them – I hadn't succumbed, not really. I hadn't done anything at all except dare to dream of Terrence Blue, the most dangerous man in Los Angeles. And the most sensuous.

He'd kissed me on the cheek when he brought me up to the hotel. "Room 342," he'd said with a grin. "I'll be sure to remember that." But he hadn't tried to come inside. He'd been a perfect gentleman.

"Tomorrow's Monday," he had said before I went in. "It's your day off. You should do something special with it."

"I don't want to do anything," I'd said.

"Suit yourself. But I want you to know – you have the option."

I'd spent a few hours just walking around the room, in shock. The Blue Tower was everything they'd said it was and more. I'd never even dreamed of luxury like this. Satin sheets, four-poster beds, a balcony with a view over Los Angeles, twenty-four inch plasma television screens, a minibar stocked with the finest liquors a girl like me could want. *If my mother could see me here,* I thought – with a pang – *she wouldn't believe her eyes.*

If my mother could see me here.

The thought filled me with shame. Me, here, in a hotel room that probably cost as much per night as a whole course of chemotherapy. I had a wild urge to steal something, anything – the art on the walls, the beautiful mahogany carvings on the mantlepiece – to pawn it that very night and run to my mother with the cash in hand and tell her to make one last attempt, one last-ditch try, to get out of that hospice. To survive.

Stupid girl, I'd chided myself then. Believing in last-minute miracles. Believing that any good could come out of a place like this.

I was here for one reason and one reason only. To find out what happened to Rita. To expose this place as the evil it was.

I walked through the room, letting my fingertips trace the satin on the bed. I took a bath in the Jacuzzi and tried to watch the sweat, the sickness, the shame off my

The Blue Room (The Blue Room Vol. 1)

skin. But they'd got it sticking to me good. Even after an hour in the tub, scrubbing myself fervently, I couldn't stop smelling Terrence Blue on my skin.

And now I'd dreamed about him.

A knock comes at my door. Breakfast – this early? On my day off? I groan as I pull on a lilac silk dressing gown and go to the door.

"Good morning, miss. Courtesies of Terrence Blue," the maid holds out a silver platter. "He says to spend your day off wisely." She looks up at me. "A car's waiting downstairs to take you to the airport."

I look down in shock at the platter. There it is, a first class ticket to Los Vegas.

My mouth drops open.

Does he know?

No, he can't know. He thinks I'm like the other girls, that I want to go squander all my winnings in the slot machines, that I want to get drunk and party. Maybe he thinks a weekend in Vegas among all those high rollers will loosen me up, make me more willing to..

I shake my head.

He has *no* idea that what I want most in Vegas can't be found coming out of any slot machine.

Before lunchtime, I'm taking a taxi up to the Sweet Ranch Hospice. I've taken off all my makeup, worn my most girlish dress.

I'm here to see my mother.

Her face lights up when she sees me. Even under the sickness, there's a woman there, a woman capable of such incredible joy when she's near the people she loves. Not even cancer can ravage that smile, that smile of pure love. Of real love – true love – not the sordid fake affection you buy and sell at the Blue Room. Seeing her, in this simple place – the only hospice we can afford for her – makes me feel ashamed at the luxury I've left behind.

"Honey!" Her voice is still strong. "I've missed you so much."

"I've missed you too, Mom."

I wish I could be with her all the time. I wish I didn't have to leave.

"How's your new job?"

I flush. "It's good, I guess. They pay me pretty well." I feel a sudden burst of pride when I'm able to leave a stack of bills on her table. "I want you to order anything you want, ok? Order delivery from the finest

The Blue Room (The Blue Room Vol. 1)

restaurant in town. All the dessert you want."

"The good life, huh?" Her laugh is a croak, and brings tears to my eyes. "Careful, Staci, you know I can't have too much fat. I might get a heart attack."

The humor is black, but it binds us together.

"You found an apartment yet?"

"Actually – the club puts the girls up. In a hotel they own."

My mother''s brow furrows. "That's pretty unusual, honey."

"It's normal for them. It's how they keep an eye on us – make sure we're working out, practicing, eating all our vegetables."

"They're not..." she sighs. "They're not making you do anything you want to do, are they?"

"No, Mommy," I place my hand against her cheek. "Don't worry. I'm totally in control." Involuntarily, I summon Terrence to mind again. I shiver at the thought of him.

"You be careful, hear?" She pulls me closer. "These places, some of them. They exist to make money off the backs of beautiful, naïve girls like you."

"I'm not naïve."

"You know that world – it isn't all glitz and glamour."

"I know, Mom." I've known that since before I was born.

"Any boys out there – to keep you on the straight and narrow?"

"One..." I answer in spite of myself. "But I don't think straight and narrow is exactly his scene."

She looks worried again. "I don't like the sound of him."

"Don't worry," I tell her, patting her hand. "I have my head screwed on straight."

"There are mistakes I don't want you making."

"Don't worry, Mom. You raised a responsible girl." I try not to let the tears fall. "One who knows how to be careful."

Now my mother is smiling again. She's positively beaming.

"I know, Staci. When I see you coming in here, looking the way you look – you're so beautiful. Not just outside, but inside. You're radiant. Healthy. Happy. I'm so proud of the way you've grown up. I know it hasn't always been easy for us, but you've never let the

The Blue Room (The Blue Room Vol. 1)

challenges you faced set you back. You know they'll only ever help you get stronger. You've seen so much, done so much. And I believe you could have the life I...."

I never got to have.

But she won't say that. Not for a second. She won't ever admit that having me ruined her life, ruined her dreams.

"The truth is, though," my mom smiles. "Despite everything. Despite the hardship, the difficulties, the motels...I wouldn't have had it any other way."

"That's crazy." Of course she would have. She could have been a star, a diva, a millionaire. She could have had it all, made it big. Instead she made that one huge mistake.

"Having you..." She beams up at me. "That was my dream. That was worth it. And I wouldn't trade you for all the stardom, all the fame and fortune, all the success in the world. I got my dream coming true. Every time I look at you, I'm reminded of that. But I want you to have it easier than I did, Staci. I want you to have *everything*. Love and success. A family and a career. And I worry that Hollywood, LA, that world – it's not the place to get that everything."

Maybe she'd rather me to go to law school, business school, med school. Something safe. Something that would put me on the track to success.

But I've always known that I have to sing. I've always known that my future, my fate, is onstage. It's in the Atussi blood.

"Promise me something," she whispers, and I know whatever it is, whatever she wants, I'll make that promise to her.

"Of course, Mom. Anything."

"If you find a man – make sure he's a good man. Don't settle for anything less. He can be poor, he can be shy, he can have too-big ears or be a little bit awkward at remembering your anniversary. But make sure he's a *good* man. One who treats you right. And if you can't find one that you like, promise me, honey, you'll take up with no man at all. Never take up with a man who isn't good – you promise me that?"

I think of Terrence, again, and I'm almost ashamed of how far I almost let things go, how stupid I almost let him make me be. I think of him, and once more my thighs clench together involuntarily in memory

The Blue Room (The Blue Room Vol. 1)

of the pleasure he gave me. I remember screaming his name in my dreams and I blush.

But I say nothing. I take my mother into my arms and kiss her, hold her, make her the promise that I'm also making to myself.

"I promise, Mom."

I mean it.

Chapter 6

I don't have too long to stay at my mother's side. My return ticket was for 5:30, and I know I have to get a good night's sleep at the Blue Tower if I want to do a halfway decent job at the club tomorrow. Not that I'm sure whether or not I want to. Doing a good job means that a lot of men will be clamoring to spend the night with me – and I'm not sure I'm ready for that yet.

Could I do it? If I had to. If it was the only way I could keep my cover. My virginity was just a concept, after all – sex was just an act, wasn't it? And Rita – I had to find out what happened to her. If she was even still alive. If she needed my help. If Rita was in danger somewhere, I'd have to do whatever it took to get her out safely. And if that meant making men like Angus happy, I guess that's what I'd have to do.

The idea still fills me with revulsion – and anger. What is it about a woman's body that made the most

The Blue Room (The Blue Room Vol. 1)

powerful men – because the powerful were always men, aren't they? – lose all control like that? What is it about this skin, these bones, this collection of flesh that I live and breathe in, this part of myself, that men thinks belongs to them, just because they want to do things to it? Don't I have more to offer them than my pound of flesh?

I want to be sick. I don't doubt what Terrence says – that the Blue Room is one of the most powerful places in the world. It's where deals are made and broken – over bodies like mine. Over the backs of women like me. I retch the whole plane ride home, thinking about it.

No, I decide. If I'm going to have sex, it's going to be for me, because I want to, because I love and trust someone. Not because some rich guy with a hard-on thinks I owe him one just for existing while male. My mother is right. I'm better off with no man at all than with a man who treats me like a piece of meat.

But could I pretend? Just for a little while? Just if it meant getting Rita home safely?

I try not to think about it. I tell myself I don't have to decide just now. That I'll be able to hold the wolves from the door just a little longer.

By the time I get back to the Blue Tower, I'm exhausted, physically and emotionally. My day off hasn't exactly been a vacation. I make my way to the service entrance, and am surprised to find the maid I knew that morning looking at me in shock.

"What are you doing here, miss?"

"Going...home?" I venture.

"Miss, the Blue Room girls take the guest entrance – like everyone else."

"But we're...service, aren't we?" I mean, we get the luxury, the amenities, the perks – but we're just working girls, after all.

"Terrence is insistent. All our girls live like guests, here."

The public entrance. The shiny new lobby. Terrence wants us all out in public. Pretending to be famous actresses, movie stars, society ladies. Pretending like we're not glorified prostitutes. But that's all LA is, isn't it? Pretend.

So I strut into the front lobby, my head held high, and pretend like I own the place.

All the while, I wonder. *Do they know*? The other people here – the businessmen drinking in the

The Blue Room (The Blue Room Vol. 1)

lobby, the matrons with their tiny Maltese dogs sitting and waiting to check in – do they know who I really am? What I really do? How much I don't belong here with them?

When I get to my room, I'm surprised to find that someone's been in. There's a whole bunch of files that weren't here before, all in beautifully monogrammed stationary. "Breakfast. Manners. Exercise. Language Skills. Facial. Waxing. Sauna."

Apparently, they want me to learn conversational Mandarin and Arabic, fluent French, art history, and the political history of the Balkans. It's a better education than I ever got at Briar Valley Community College, that's for sure.

I'm almost excited.

The menus, though, make my heart sink. Prescribed diets – all carrot sticks and celery – with precise times to eat and drink every day of the week. Eyebrow tweezing is scheduled, as are scrubs, waxing, and something unappetizingly referred to as a "mud rub".

This isn't going to be easy.

On the top of the files is a handwritten note, in a

style so elegant it looks like calligraphy.

> *See me at once. 2nd Floor, Room 202.*
> *Josephine Walters (Mrs.).*

I begin to wonder about Josephine Walters (Mrs.). At once, I form a mental image of her: something like the formidable madam from *Gone With the Wind* and the stern matron of a girls' boarding school. I immediately know she's behind all of this – from the Mandarin to the tweezing. And, all of a sudden, I'm terrified.

It's with great trepidation that I force my way down the hallway and into the elevator. Whoever this Josephine Walters (Mrs.) is, I have a feeling she isn't going to like me. Mandarin and Arabic, let alone a 24/7 beauty routine, aren't exactly my forte. I didn't exactly grow up going to finishing school. Sure, I'd have loved to learn the socio-political history of the Balkans, but I was a bit too busy flipping burgers to pay for our by-the-night motels to do more than scrawl out the answers to my school assignments.

I'm not, in other words, high-class courtesan material.

But the woman I see sitting behind the desk in

The Blue Room (The Blue Room Vol. 1)

the sparsely decorated, briskly efficient office in room 202 hardly looks like a high-class courtesan *or* a frightening matriarch. Small, wiry, with black hair pinned in a prim bun and square-rimmed black glasses sitting neatly on her pert little nose, Josephine Walter (Mrs.) looks like a businesswoman, not a madam.

"Good evening, Miss Atussi." She shakes my hand as briskly as if I were here on a job interview.

"You wanted to see me?"

"Yes." Her eyes dart to the desk, and I see she's got my file before her. "I've just been going over what I have on you. I see you have some college."

"An associate's degree..." I say. "I wanted to go to a four-year program, but money..."

She's moved on. "Performance experience, that's good. Local plays. Amateur dramatics. Church choir."

She raises an eyebrow.

"Service experience, you've got plenty of."

Flipping burgers, she means?

"I worked for a dentist during college," I said. Like somehow working for a dentist was more respectable than flipping burgers. Like somehow flipping burgers was something to be ashamed of – when

I was applying to work as a prostitute.

"So, you can work with people."

"I mostly did filing," I say. "Calling in for records."

"I see. So fresh." She gives me the once-over and I don't even have the foggiest idea what she's thinking. "So fresh and young. Stand up."

I stand up.

"Walk."

I walk.

"No, no, no." Her voice is low but clear. "It's all wrong. You walk too fast – too much energy. Too bubbly. Like you're someone's kid sister."

"But I'm only..." I automatically protest.

"I don't care how old you are. You're over eighteen, aren't you? You're a woman, not a girl. These are worldly men we cater to here. Men who want women who know how to feel comfortable and assured in their own skin. Who feel luxurious in their own bodies. You see the starlets, the supermodels, these men take on dates to events, premieres, launch parties? They may be young, but they've seen the world. They're self-assured, confident, and sophisticated beyond their years. Not

The Blue Room (The Blue Room Vol. 1)

jejune girls-next-door."

I almost flush.

"Well if they've got starlets and models as girlfriends," I can't stop myself from being sarcastic, "I don't see what they need *us* for, anyhow."

Josephine Walters (Mrs.) shakes her head. "I imagine a girl like you would know more about the psychology of the opposite sex than that."

I'm not sure if that's an insult or a compliment, so I force myself to keep my mouth shut. But I can't bite my tongue. "I've been busy," I said. "Earning money. Supporting my mom. Doesn't give me a lot of time to date around."

"Then I'll summarize it for you in a nutshell. Clearly you like things done quickly. Men at the Blue Room –they want it here, and they want it all. They want the illusion. They may have famous and beautiful companions outside of the Blue Room, but that's nothing, *nothing*, to what they can have in here. Here is where they can let their wildest dreams, their most depraved fantasies, their most unorthodox desires come true. And the girls at the Blue Room will satisfy these desires. They will go wherever those men take them."

Is that where Rita went? Wherever some man took her?

"So, you mean sex." I know I should hold my tongue, but I can't. This place – this woman – are filling me with rage.

"Please! So vulgar!" She raises her head at me. "This isn't Nevada. Prostitution is illegal here. We would never, *ever* formally encourage our girls to sleep with clients."

I nod.

"What happens between you and our clients, romantically or otherwise, is between the two of you."

"I understand," I say. I read between the lines. *We want you to sleep with them, but if something goes wrong, then it's your problem, kid. You're on your own.*

Josephine Walters (Mrs.) smiles. "Men come to the Blue Room because we offer them the best. We offer them a place where they can get their needs and desires met. In other words, this is the place where they can get what they need – and what they can't get anywhere else." Her lips are like rubies. "Clear enough for you, Miss Atussi?"

Chapter 7

I'm sure what to expect next. My experience with Josephine Walter (Mrs.) leaves me shaken. The way she speaks about the things I would have to do – why, it was if she's talking about mergers and acquisitions: something formal and businesslike and utterly expected! I can hardly believe the meaning behind her words. Even after a few days in the world of the Blues, I'm utterly bewildered by how...normal it all seems. Having sex for money, in the world of the Blue Room, is a boring everyday occurrence.

I wonder for a second if I'm doing the right thing. If there isn't some other way to find Rita, some better way, some way that doesn't require me to sacrifice my virginity in the process. But I know now that I'm Rita's last hope. The police never care about girls like Rita – strippers, hookers, whatever you want to call them. And if the clientele here at the Blue Room is as powerful as I'm starting to understand it is, then the last

Kailin Gow

thing any policeman in this town wants to do is to piss them off, ask too many questions. That's just the way things are in this town. The rich get richer and the poor get – whatever it was Rita got.

I've got to find out what happened to her. I've got to find out why.

I sit alone in my room, catching my breath. I'm almost tempted to smoke a cigarette, but I'm pretty sure if I do Josephine Walters is going to descend on me like a hawk and give me a lecture about spoiling my teeth and skin. They treat us right, here, that's for sure. Like prized cows, fattened for the slaughter.

From my suitcase I take out a little ribbon, a locket dangling on the end of it. Rita bought it for me a few weeks after she started working at the Blue Room.

"You work so hard," she said to me. "You're so beautiful. You deserve a little something for yourself."

I remember how I stared at it in amazement. That silver must have cost her a fortune – that's what I said. I remember telling her how I couldn't accept a gift like that – how I couldn't understand how a girl like Rita could make so much money, so fast.

"Thank you."

The Blue Room (The Blue Room Vol. 1)

"Don't thank me. Thank Mr. X."

She smiled at me sadly.

"It's my very first spend," she said. "I wanted the first money I earned at the Blue Room to go to somebody other than myself. It makes me feel better that way..."

"You don't have to..."

"Do you *know* how big my student loans are?" She swallowed. "My mom and dad – they co-signed my med school loans. But my dad lost his job – and they're gonna lose the house, too, if they're saddled with my debt." She inhaled sharply. "I'm going to do what I have to do. I got them into this mess. I'll get them out."

The first night I wore the locket, I thought I'd sell it. I was desperate at the time, making barely more than minimum wage at my receptionist job, and all I could think of was how much I could pawn it for. It was so tempting. How many hours of my shift would it get me? Fifteen? Forty? Enough for a whole night's sleep at a time? Enough for fifteen minutes of Rita's time at the Blue Room.

But after hearing what she said about it being her first purchase, I couldn't sell it. I couldn't bring myself to. Rita had wanted to do something nice for me – she'd given it to me – she'd bound us together.

Even today I feel responsible for taking it. What would have happened if I'd insisted, if I'd refused to take it at all, if I hadn't looked at that locket and seen dollar signs, and instead told her that what she was doing was dangerous, insisted that she stop?

She might be with me, still, in our apartment. Doctor Rita – or almost. Successful, happy, paying off her med-school loans the old-fashioned way. But such an imagining – I don't have time for hypotheticals. I don't have time for nice little alternatives. All I know is that Rita was my best friend, like a sister I've never had, and now there's a bigger chance than I want to admit that she's dead.

So I finger the locket. And I tell myself I'll do what I have to do. Virginity's just a social construct, after all; sex is just a thing you do with your body. Sex is just an act. Finding Rita is another act. I tell myself that's all I need to know.

So I sit down with my schedule, and I see I've only got five minutes of reminiscing before

7:00 pm. Facial.

The Blue Room (The Blue Room Vol. 1)

7:30 pm. Makeover.

I don't even have to go anywhere. A small, quiet brunette raps at my door within seconds of the clock hitting seven; she covers me with poultices and ointments and scrubs which probably cost more than a whole month's salary at Dr. O'Donovan's office.

As they plump and primp me, I start to feel sick again. It's not just the thought of having sex with someone I don't love. People do that often enough, I guess. It's being surrounded by so much money. It's the same feeling I had when Rita gave me that necklace. The Creme de Mer ointments, the Clarins creams, that distinctive perfume that you know only oligarch's wives can afford – all of the smells, the tastes, the sensations, remind me that everyone around me can buy and sell me in a heartbeat. The kind of money that could save my mother's life? That's just a tip scrawled on a credit card bill for one night on the town.

It makes me sick, at first.

And then I start thinking.

One jar of these creams. Sell it on ebay for $200. Ten of those – that's a long way towards covering Mom's hospital debt. Pocket a necklace or two – that's a round *of chemo.*

A stack of Washingtons by the bedside? That's an experimental, aggressive treatment. The kind that might save someone's life. The kind that last-ditch attempts are made of.

And then it hits me.

I'm like Rita.

I want that money just as much.

Everyone around me is buying me, selling me, like I'm a toy. Terrence Blue wants to buy and sell me. At once I hate everyone around me, all these people who think they own me, who think they know what I'm like. The people who thought they owned Rita, too, before they got tired of owning her – whatever that means.

If I'm gonna be bought and sold, I'd better be the one doing the selling. I want to make a profit on my own back.

All these people – Terrence Blue, Angus the businessman – I don't want to just *fuck* them. I want to *be* them. I want to have the power they have. I want to buy and sell and trade with the best of them, rip them off and send the proceeds to my mother in Nevada.

Whoever my first patron was, no matter how

The Blue Room (The Blue Room Vol. 1)

ugly, no matter how repulsive, I resolved to screw him. In more ways than one. I was going to do this *my* way. Just like Terrence.

As the girl leaned over me and started putting make-up on my face, changing me into a creature of unrecognizable beauty, a girl who hardly looked like *me* at all, I thought of all the girls I knew back home who lost their virginities for far less romantic reason. At parties with guys, in the back of fraternity houses, out of peer pressure, out of fear of being the last virgin at our school.

I wouldn't just do it for money. I'd do it for knowledge. For power.

One day, I swore to myself, I was going to walk into a room with Terrence Blue and buy and sell this place from right out under him.

"Here, Miss Atussi!" The girl rolled out a mirror to show me what she'd done.

I couldn't believe the sight of me. I was dressed in a form-fitting mint-colored minidress, the heels on my feet sparkly and diamond-encrusted. My hair was smooth and sleek in a pageboy style; my lips were glossed and my eyes were blue, pouty, smoky – the eyes of a femme fatale. I didn't look like some cheap streetwalker, I thought. If I was going to be a prostitute, I was going to be a damn expensive one.

"Sexy!" I heard Mrs. Walter's voice in the doorway. "Sexy, Miss Atussi, is more than just having expensive shoes. It's about more than how much skin you reveal. It's about how you carrying yourself. It's about how you look men in the eyes. Our Blues Girls look and act like a million bucks. Unattainable. Worthy of being won. These men are powerful men who seek out the best – like challenges. They bet on racehorses, collect artwork, stay at the nicest hotels. They want their sex to be the best experience they've had, too. If you're too easy, you're not worth it. If you play hard to get but display cnough interest in him, then you will present a challenge to him. He will want you. Make him crave you, and you will find yourself cherished."

I didn't know a lot about being alluring. But I knew a lot about pretending. Back before money was too tight for me to think about anything but work, I'd wanted to be an actress. Well, I'd act now.

My first patron wouldn't know what hit him.

"He will meet you in the hotel tonight to take

The Blue Room (The Blue Room Vol. 1)

you to dinner downstairs at Azure. Then he will follow you back up to your room after dinner to – get to know you better. If you please him enough during that time, and he stays until morning, you'll double your income. Given your – unique – status, that would net you about twenty-five thousand."

My jaw drops. "Dollars?"

"Dollars – what did you think?"

My jaw's still hanging open.

"But *only* if you impress him enough. The only thing guaranteed is dinner."

"What's the point of hiring a hooker if you don't want to sleep with her?" I can hear myself get nasty.

"This patron is selective," she says. "He wants to see if he likes you enough to take things further. His time is precious and he doesn't like to waste it."

I'm almost insulted. Not only do I have to sell my body for money – I have to convince someone I'm worth it?

"Now, you look perfect," Mrs. Walters says. "Don't mess up your makeup before he sees you. As for after – well, men like ruining a woman's makeup themselves. But let it be a man's doing – not some mess you make between now and then."

I say nothing. I'm too stunned to come up with a clever remark.

I go back to my hotel room and try to relax. I turn on the television, listen to music. I try to turn on my computer only to find that the wireless is blocked. I guess they're not too keen on us girls having any contact with the outside world while we're here.

I watch the clock tick down.

8:25...8:26...8:29.

8:30.

The doorbell rings.

Chapter 8

At once I snap to my feet. I'm on it, I tell myself. Elegant. Unattainable. Alluring.

At least until I knock over the vase on the bedside table.

"Oh, shit!" All the alluring in the world flies right out of me as I try to pick up the pieces of the vase. "Shit, shit, shit."

"Not really the reaction I was hoping for!"

Terrence Blue is standing in the doorway.

He's all dressed up – so much so it takes me a second to be sure it's really him. In the Blue Room, Terrence had gone for grunge, but now he's quite the gentleman: clean-shaven, in an impeccably tailored suit.

Surely he knows the client's coming! Or is this all part of Terrence's sick sense of humor – to try and throw me off my game when I least expect it.

"I'm sorry," I say. "It's the vase. It's probably a

Waterford or something – I'm sorry."

"No harm done." He just strolls in like he owns the place. Which, to be fair, he does. "I'll just replace it then." He picks up the pieces and starts putting them in the trashcan. "I'll get housekeeping in here while we're gone."

"Not that it isn't lovely to see you," I try to smile. "But you're kind of ruining my concentration."

"And what is it that you're concentrating on, dear Staci?"

"I'm preparing for my...uh...*work meeting*."

He shuts the door and looks me up and down. I can feel how his eyes sear into me. It feels terrifying – and good, at the same time. I'm in disarray – mentally, physically. How can this man have such an effect on me? I think I'm powerful, think I'm strong, ready for all the challenges that lie before me, and then in a heartbeat this Terrence Blue can have me up against a wall, panting, desperate.

"You look delectable, Staci. I'm sure your *work meeting* will go very well indeed. Makeovers always do a number on my girls – but you're a butterfly, now. Completely transformed. Into the glam femme fatale I always knew you were."

Before I can say anything Terrence has me up against the door, his hand moving up my inner thigh, fingering my panties.

Great, I think. The last thing I can afford right now is to ruin the expensive La Perla lace panties that were part of my *work uniform*. But Terrence has already got them soaked through. As much by the look he gives me as by his sensual touch.

The heat is overpowering. His hands against my thigh, his fingers caressing deeper, rubbing me just enough to get the blood pumping and that breath so shallow in my throat. All I know right now is – I want him. I want him so badly I'm willing to throw everything else away if he can just let me come.

And he knows it.

He knows I'm enjoying him just as much as he's enjoying me. The thrill of the chase. Combat in caresses. He knows I know it too.

"You're just as excited about me as I am about you." His breath is warm against my neck. "Your body is more talkative than you are, Staci."

"Terrence." His fingers are in all the right

places, now, moving faster and faster, bringing up my heart rate with each slow and torturous caress. It's hot, so hot, and all I want to do is tear off that expensive mint gown Mrs. Walters has bought for me. No, who am I kidding? I want him to tear it off.

"I love watching you," he whispers. "Your face." He probes deeper, and then his fingers are inside me, pressing upwards, into that rough patch of flesh that sends me wild. I'm moaning – I know that now – and I can't stop myself. I don't know if I want to. "So full of desire and passion."

He's getting rougher, now. Almost violent. But his eyes are fixed on me and I know he's listening to every beat of my heart, every sharp intake of breath. I know he knows he's going to push me exactly how far I can go – and no further. He knows my body as well as I do.

"Oh, Terrence!" I'm moaning; I'm panting; I'm heaving. They can hear me all the way down in Mrs. Walters' office. "Terrence – this – this feels so good – but..."

But my client's meant to be here already. And somehow I don't think watching me get fingered by

The Blue Room (The Blue Room Vol. 1)

Terrence Blue is the kink he signed up for.

Or maybe it is, who knows? The Blue Room's clientele seem pretty into the weird stuff.

"You have no idea what you're missing." Terrence whispers into my ears. "Such pleasure. Such wild pleasure. All yours. A body and a face like yours – your body is an instrument. Built to give, but also to receive."

At once I'm on the defensive. I'm no instrument – I'm not *built for* anything, except maybe finding out the truth about Rita. But it's hard to think about that when my mind is going blank, when my eyes are rolling back into my head, when with a shudder and a scream that feels like an explosion I'm coming onto his fingers, his hand, against his chest, crying out into his neck.

I buck a few more times and then he takes his fingers out of me, lifts them to his lips, begins to suck them dry.

The look he gives me almost makes me come a second time.

"Next time," he says, and I'm wet again just hearing it. "I'll take off your panties first. Then I'll do exactly what I just did to you – only next time, I'm going to use my tongue. And you'll come so fast – I know girls like you – on edge the way you are. It'll only take a few licks before you come so hard you won't know what hit you. But it won't be over." He wipes his lips with a handkerchief, impeccably monogrammed TJB. "I bet you can come at least four or five times in an hour. You look like it this time. And I'm going to make sure I have the chance to find out."

I can't even think.

A knock at the door slams us both out of the reverie.

"It's him!" My voice catches in my throat.

Shit. How am I going to get Terrence out of here?

I start fixing my lipstick, my hair, everything. I tell myself that this is all part of the plan – that seducing Terrence Blue is the best way to get inside the *real* back of the Blue Room, to figure out what happened to Rita and why. But why does it feel like he seduced me? And why does it feel so good?

"It's him..."

But before I can get to the door, Terrence is already there. He leans out, whispers a few words, then

The Blue Room (The Blue Room Vol. 1)

closes it again before I can say anything.

"Why did you send him away?" I ask.

My first client – and I don't even get to meet him? Terrence Blue is bad for business.

"An unnecessary distraction."

"But he's already paid!" I cry out. "Mrs. Walters says he's already paid for dinner..."

Terrence bursts out laughing. "Staci," he says. "That was housekeeping. For the vase."

"But..." the realization hits me before I finish the sentence. "My patron."

Terrence doesn't say anything. He just stares at me, with those amazing blue eyes, until I nod, slowly.

"I think you've passed the dinner test, Staci," he says. "Normally I make my decisions after dessert – but in this case – I think I will have you for the rest of the night."

I stare up at him in shock.

I'd been prepared to sleep with a patron, that much was true. I'd been prepared to sleep with someone for whom I felt nothing, not even attraction, to turn off my body and my mind and just go through the motions, like a robot. Be an actress, playing a scene with a stranger. But it hadn't occurred to me that I'd have to sleep with Terrence. Terrence for whom I felt something real, even if it was just desire.

"You're joking..." Somehow, I know he's not. "Terrence – you have to go before my client gets here."

"Don't play dumb, Staci." He grins, pinning my arms above my head as he presses against me once again. He leans in to kiss me behind the ears, which feels so good that my heart stops for a second in sheer ecstasy. I half-close my eyes, enjoying the way his tongue is probing my ears, my neck. "I'm getting through to you, Miss Atussi. That much I'm sure of." His kiss intoxicates me. "Little by little," he says. "I'm chipping away that virginal little chastity belt of yours." He applies more pressure, then his teeth, and that little bit of pain sends me over the edge. I'm moaning again, unable to stand it any longer.

"You see, I've found one of your buttons." I'm practically screaming. "You're still new enough to pleasure, that discovering it excites you. You're still so untouched, so fresh – you take such pleasure in the pleasure you feel. You can't fake how your skin heats up underneath my fingers. You can't fake how your pretty blue eyes are dilated so wide. Your body's taking over. Whatever your mind is screaming, it won't listen."

"Terrence...my dress...my hair..." I don't even know what I'm saying now.

"Sorry baby. Those things are beyond repair. It's fine. I'll pay damages." His teeth nip against my neck and leave a bruise. His smile is wicked. "I called the original client – assigned him elsewhere."

"Why would you do that?" My mouth falls open. Against myself I'm thinking of the money, of what it could do for my mother.

"Don't worry," he said. "You'll still get paid. I'll see to that. But I don't know what Mrs. Walters was thinking booking you with him for the night. Although I can see how he could have gotten a whiff of you from that little performance you did onstage the other night."

"He seems...specific," I say, thinking of how carefully Mrs. Walters and the others made me up.

I'd rather him than Terrence. At least then I don't have to worry about falling for him.

"He likes that glamorous look. The sex bomb you pretend to be. "

"Well, then I'll pretend to be experienced for

him," I say. "Isn't that my job. To fulfill men's fantasies."

"Not his," Terrence looks grave. "Look – Staci," his voice is almost tender. "The stuff he likes – this guy is extreme. And he wants extreme things. To do to girls and to be done to him. There's a reason he pays as much as he does. But the stuff he'll ask you to do – it will take a toll. Even among the Blue Girls, several refuse to see him. After what he's done to some of the girls."

Girls like Rita?

Now I'm more curious than ever to meet him.

"What does he do to them?"

"He's one of our best patrons at the club," says Terrence, as if that settles it. "What he wants, he gets."

"So he can have his way with any girl?" The hairs on the back of my neck stand up. "What if they say no?"

His smile is dark. "They never say no."

Chapter 9

"I want to see him," I say.

It's the most dangerous thing I've ever said, but right now, I'm sure it's what I want. This man – whoever he is – sounds like someone who might have known Rita. Who might have killed her. No, I won't let myself think that way. All I know is – he might know where Rita is. And right now, that's good enough for me.

Part of me, too, knows that it'll be easier this way. To do sick, strange things with a stranger won't shake me nearly as much as taking money for sex with Terrence Blue. I'm not afraid of getting hurt.

"I want to protect you," he says.

I want to laugh in his face.

"*You* want to protect *me?*"

Like he hasn't grown up in the lap of luxury. Like he hasn't grown up with everything he's ever wanted. He thinks I haven't met prostitutes before?

Pimps? Men who beat up women? When you grow up in the one-night-cheap motels of Las Vegas, you learn pretty early on that you have to protect yourself. I've been beaten up before. Back when I worked the cash register, drunks would try to get fresh all the time. And he thinks he's going to protect me? Ridiculous.

I'm going to protect myself. And Rita, too. If she's still alive.

"Why?"

"If he can have whatever he wants," I say, "he's going to have me sooner or later. And I don't want to waste time. Maybe I'll change my mind tomorrow. You might want to sell me off while I'm still ready, willing, and able."

"I told him you were so new – we didn't have all your paperwork filled out yet. Confidentiality agreements. Security checks. STD testing."

"Confidentiality agreements?"

"This patron is discreet. Not that he needs paperwork to keep people quiet. This guy has a lot of people who – ah – shut people up as necessary."

I'm starting to get nervous. But I didn't come to the Blue Room to back out. My intuition tells me that

The Blue Room (The Blue Room Vol. 1)

this guy is the guy I want.

"I want to know who he is."

"You don't," says Terrence. "You're better off not knowing. We have a lot of people who come into the Blue Room. Celebrities, princes, billionaires, politicians. People powerful enough to make those disappear whom they perceive as a threat. Many of our girls don't even know his name. He likes it that way."

Did he make Rita disappear? The question has filled my brain so entirely I can't think of anything else.

"You can at least tell me what he's into," I say. "I want to be prepared."

"He's rough," said Terrence. "Dominant."

"I can handle that."

"Are you sure you can?"

He takes my hand and pushes me onto the bed.

"When you can't even handle this?"

He gets on top of me. He's straddling me.

"He's not going to take his time with you. He's not going to kiss you gently, make you wet. He runs the world. He hasn't got time for that."

I can't help myself. Again I'm turned on – so turned on I can't move.

"Don't move," he says.

"I'm not – oh!"

His tongue is down between my thighs, working its way upwards.

He finds what he's looking for. I arch my back. The pleasure is so intense I can't stand it. My panties are down somewhere around my ankles; his face is buried between my legs; his tongue is licking me over and over, probing deep, reenacting the motions of his fingers earlier.

He's right. I can't handle it.

"You're delicious," he murmurs, his breath intoxicating me as it ripples between my legs.

I scream his name over and over when I come.

"That's one," he whispers. He strips the dress from me, pulls it onto the floor.

"I want to eat you all night."

I tell myself I'm doing this for Rita. I'm preparing myself for the moment when I'll have to meet this man, have to pretend I know what I'm doing.

Before I find the truth.

Right now, I'm lost in him.

He kisses every part of me, nipping at the most

The Blue Room (The Blue Room Vol. 1)

sensitive areas, driving me wild. His tongue finds places I didn't even know were part of me – patches of skin that under him are nothing but nerves.

"More..." My voice is rough and hungry. "Don't stop."

"A second course?"

He's explored every part of me. Soon he's stripped down to his underwear; soon I'm exploring him, too, with my lips, just as he has explored me.

At last I can't stand it any longer.

I tell him exactly what I want him to do to me.

"Oh, Staci," he groans. "I wish I could. But Mrs. Walters would have my head."

"What do you mean?"

"There's a price on virginity here," he said. "Stupid, isn't it. When we both know what you're capable of. When we both know how depraved your desires are, how deep they go – in your own mind. But that *technicality* is worth a pretty penny to several of our patrons.

"And – this patron? Does *he* want a virgin?"

"He shouldn't," Terrence looks faintly disgusted. "The stuff he's into – it's not exactly how most girls want their first time to be."

"I'm not most girls," I say.

"He likes virgins," Terrence says. "He especially likes *experienced* virgins. Who know how to please a man. But who give him that little ego-boost – of having him been their first."

"Then I guess you'll have to leave." I'm trying to play sassy – but deep down I don't want him to go. I want to stay in his arms until morning. I've come three times tonight, and still I want more. He's awakened a hunger in me I didn't know I had. A knowledge of my own body, my own strength.

I should feel conquered, I think. Seduced. Instead, I feel in control. Powerful. Like I'm recognizing a part of myself that I didn't even know existed.

"You're going to have to make up for that somehow," I say. I'm laughing, even joking as I say it, but I'm proud of the power I have over him when I see the desire cross his face in a smile. "If you can't be inside me..."

"I'll have to find some other way to make you moan."

We understand each other perfectly.

The Blue Room (The Blue Room Vol. 1)

But when the clock strikes three in the morning, Terrence gets up.

"Sorry, darling," he said. "I have an unbroken streak of never spending the night with any woman."

I pretend like it's okay.

After all, I need time to myself. To recover. And to eat. I haven't had dinner and it hits me all at once that I'm starving.

"Next time," I try to make it a joke. "Take me out to dinner first."

"That'd be a challenge," he says. "I'm not sure I could be with you in any setting when I couldn't reach up between your legs whenever I wanted. I don't know if I'd be able to stand it."

And with that, he leaves me.

The next morning, I hardly have time to reflect on what's going on. There's no beauty treatment listed on the schedule, but the daily handwritten letter slipped under my door at some insane hour says

8:00. Mixology. Ben.

Ben, I learn, is an affable bartender who works in the Blue Room. He shows up at my hotel room with a bottle of Courvoisier in each hand.

"Sorry it's so early," he says "I bet you're wondering who on earth drinks at a time like this?

"Can't we start with mimosas," I say. "After all, it's not even brunch."

"You know what they say." He grins. "It's five-o-clock *somewhere* in the world."

His task, he explains, is to teach me drinks. Not just how to make them – that would be too easy. But how to identify wine and fine spirits by their taste, and how to identify men's tastes by just looking at them.

"The idea is that a good bartender knows what the customer wants before he orders it," says Ben. "My ex-boyfriend, he used to say he could tell the cocktail order *before* the customer entered, just by the perfume his female companion was wearing. But that's pretty rare. Still, it's a gift. And learning about fine wines and liqueurs makes you that much more desirable as a companion." He looks apologetic.

"Sorry – that's kind of gross, isn't it?"

I laugh out loud. For the first time, someone in The Blue Room is talking like a real, normal person, not a character out of *Eyes Wide Shut*.

The Blue Room (The Blue Room Vol. 1)

"What?"

"You're the only person here who hasn't acted like this is normal."

He rolls his eyes. "I'm not going to pretend I'm not in that world," he said. "But it's easier for me if I hold onto myself in the process." His gaze turns dark. "You know – everyone is for sale here," he says. "Whether they want to be or not."

I wonder who has sold him, and when.

"I'm prepared to accept that," I say.

"Why?"

He's so nice, so warm, so trustworthy-seeming, that I almost tell him about Rita on the spot. But I think better of it. I can't trust anybody just yet. Not Ben. Not Terrence. Not even myself.

"There are worse things than sex," I say. I think of my mother in her hospital bed. "There are worse ways to sell yourself."

He nods, and for a second his stare grows melancholy.

He's seen things, I think.

"Come on," he says. "Let's start with the wines. Maybe if we get tipsy by the afternoon, it'll make your *5 pm.* more appealing."

I look at the schedule. *5 pm. Basics of the Global Economy.*

"My community college never had this stuff," I joke. "Guess I'm finally getting an education."

"Careful, Staci." His voice is low. "There's some things here nobody ever wants to learn."

Chapter 10

It is going to be a special night. That much I learn from the handwritten note Mrs. Walters slips under my door at 7 pm. There is to be no client tonight. Instead, I am going to be going to the Blue Room to learn how things worked as, as she puts it, a "silent observer." I understand at once what she means. *No more punching and kicking like last time.* I'm going to learn how the other girls – the *real* girls – perform. I'm going to know my place and keep my mouth shut.

"Don't worry," Ben smiles gently at me. "I'll be there. Serving drinks. That's all I do...now." The *now* is final and I wonder how much of Ben was really for sale. "I'll keep an eye out for anyone sketchy."

I'm not sure how to feel. Part of me is nervous – it's one thing to be one-on-one with a client, quite another to be peacocking around in front of several of the Blue Room's most important, most notable clients.

Trying to compete with the other girls there. Who am I kidding – I'm nobody's competition. These girls have been in the business for months or years. They've been whipped into shape by Mrs. Walters – and those that haven't have been kicked to the curb long-since. I'm going to be the newbie. The bottom on the totem pole. Fresh meat. It's been like that every job I ever worked in Vegas and LA alike. Last on, first off. That's what they say.

"The Never Knights are playing tonight," says Ben. "So it's not going to be quite like usual Apparently Danny Blue has been pushing to give the Blue Room a better image."

"Who's Danny?"

"Terrence's half-brother," Ben explains. "He's not like Terrence. I mean – he used to be, from what I hear, but now he's a one-woman man. A Never Knight man, at that. He's sworn off his bachelor days – and his old way of doing things. If he had his way the Blue Room would be shut down completely, or turned into a more conventional theater or music venue. He's weirded out by the whole sex thing."

"I can see why."

The Blue Room (The Blue Room Vol. 1)

Ben grins. "He's one of the good ones, this Danny. He used to be in the Never Knights. But since his father got sick he's been taking a more managerial role. Hanging up the whole guitar. Poor guy. He never wanted any of this, from what I hear. Just to teach music in California and play his guitar. But he figured – better him than Terrence."

Better him than Terrence. I think longingly of last night. I can just about deal with one Blue boy in my life – but *two*? I sigh. Good thing Danny has a girlfriend – because I couldn't withstand the advances of another one.

When we arrive at the Blue Room, the curtains are drawn tight around the stage. It's a huge stage – it could fit a whole Broadway cast on it, I think – but tonight it's a more intimate setting, and the deep velvet curtains are tight around the band.

I sigh involuntarily.

It could have been me, I think. It was me – for one night, at least. I had my shot. But now I knew I was needed elsewhere. For more intimate performances.

I'm prepared to hate Never Knight. A beautiful rock-star's daughter making her own name for herself –

yeah, right. More likely she'd been funded by Daddy's money and fame. I can't imagine her ever having it difficult in her whole life. Daddy had probably bought her a guitar by the time she was out of the womb.

But once the Never Knights started to play, I can't deny that Neve is good. Very good. She has a raw sexuality – but more than that, she has a real sense of mischief, of *fun*. Like she is enjoying herself up there. She's just singing for herself and for her bandmates, not for any of the men. She isn't selling anything. She isn't playing a role. She is just herself – powerful and fierce, and fiercely talented.

I am won over.

The rest of the band is just as good. The guitarist – "Danny's replacement," whispers Ben into my ear – is a tiny girl with an enormous pink bob and equally large saucer-green eyes, marked clearly in black liner. Her leather pants fit perfectly; her T-shirt is torn, showing off her perfect abs. She's fierce, too.

Neve is a vision. Her silver dress shows off her long tanned legs, her curvaceous body. All the guys are staring at her. Including Terrence. My jealousy comes back.

The Blue Room (The Blue Room Vol. 1)

Must be easy, I think. To be so sexy for yourself. To not have to put on a performance just for someone else.

"Hey, sexy!" I flinch as I hear Terrence approach Neve as she gets offstage.

"Hey, creepy," she rolls her eyes at him before jumping into Danny's arms, kissing him so violently that I feel ashamed of my earlier envy. Neve's clearly besotted with Danny – and he with her.

The crowd's going wild for their performance. They cheer, scream, and shout.

But what they don't do is stand.

It takes me a second to figure out why.

People at the Blue Room want to stay in the dark.

I decide to sneak backstage. From there, I reason, I'll be able to get a better view. Maybe one of the audience members tonight is my mysterious client – the one who, I'm sure, knows what happened to Rita.

I tiptoe backstage, ignoring Ben's whispered protestations.

"Hey!"

One of the band-members passes me.

"Hey, yourself."

He's got big brown eyes and a charming, even innocent smile.

"Have a beer!"

I offer him one from my platter.

"Sorry," he says. "Under 21."

I look at him in shock. Of all the rules that are being broken here, I didn't expect *that* to be the one people objected to.

"Seriously?"

He smiles bashfully at me.

Before I can ask him if he's sure, his band-mate – a tall, lanky redhead with a carefree air about him– grabs it and downs it.

"Luc may care," he grins widely at me. "But I sure don't."

"Steve's above the law," Luc rolls his eyes.

So's everyone here.

"We're gonna go meet some girls!"

Something about the way Steve says it stops me dead in my tracks. These two boys – they can't be more than twenty – and they're already seeking out prostitutes like us?

The Blue Room (The Blue Room Vol. 1)

Prostitutes like me.

I'm almost ashamed. The thought that one of them could buy and sell me makes me feel sick. They're both handsome, but in the moment I can't be attracted to either of them. They're just clients, after all.

"If you want to arrange a meeting with a Blue girl..." My voice is stilted and cold. Like Mrs. Walters.

"A Blue girl? What's that?" Luc's eyes are so wide.

"She means a groupie, stupid. Don't you?"

A groupie. A nice, normal girl. One who wants to sleep with a rock star. And who doesn't get paid. Who's in it for the fun.

"Come have a drink with us!" Luc smiles. "Well, I'll have an ice-tea, but..."

"I can't," I say. "I'm working."

"When do you get off work?"

I can't tell them the truth. I *never* get off work.

"I can't," I say. "I'm waiting for someone."

I look over at Terrence to see his eyes are only for Neve.

The others pick up on it, and I curse my inability to hide it.

"Join the club, uh..."

"Staci."

"Staci." Steve grins again. "Me, I'm a player – I'm not going to *deny* that, but I have my limits. Terrence Blue has no limits. In number of women or in...the depths of his depravity." He winks. "I hope you're into the kinky stuff."

I hope they don't see me blushing.

"Terrence the Terror." Luc sighs.

"You know him, then?"

"We know Danny. We're friends," says Luc. Then, "kind of."

"Kind of?" I ask.

"I appear to be the only straight man in the world utterly immune to Neve's charms," Steve laughs. "I mean – I love her as a friend, but thinking about her romantically is like thinking about a sister or something...Luc didn't feel the same way."

Luc looks embarrassed.

"Oh," I stutter. "I'm sorry, I didn't mean to..."

"Ancient history," Luc says with difficulty.

"Anyway, Luc's got Riley now."

"I have not!"

The Blue Room (The Blue Room Vol. 1)

"Our guitarist. She's getting *all* of his attention. Not everyone could step in into Danny's shoes, but she sure has...I'm sorry. What did you say your name was?"

"Staci." I shake his hand. "Big fan."

"A *groupie*?" He's teasing now.

"Sort of," I say.

"How can you be a *sort of* groupie?" His language is aggressive, but the boyish smile makes it clear that Steve's just a puppy.

Not like some of the men here.

What am I going to say? *I'm the kind of groupie you pay.*

"I only sleep with rock stars I really, *really* like," I try to tease back.

"And?" Steve's eyes are saucers.

"And I haven't found one yet."

It takes me a second before I realize I've accidentally let it slip that I'm a virgin.

"So what are you doing here, then?"

Oh, nothing. Hooking. Trying to solve my best friend's murder.

"I need the money."

Also true.

"You can't work somewhere a bit less – sketchy?"

"Not at this money." It's nice to laugh about it. "Sketch is expensive."

"What else do you do?"

"I sing." I say it so confidently, like I'm not talking to a world-famous rock star.

"No shit. You good?"

"Yeah," I figure I'll put a little swagger in it. "I'm pretty fucking awesome, actually."

This impresses them.

"Send me a demo sometime, okay?" Steve slips his businesscard into my hand. "We want to expand our own label."

"Is that what you say to all the girls you're trying to sleep with."

"Nah," Steve says, just as he catches the eye of a beautiful pair of twins at the bar. "Just the ones I really, *really* like." He kisses me lightly on the cheek. "See ya!"

Chapter 11

The next few days fly by in a haze. By day, I'm on a strict kale-and-vitamin-pills-diet, something I'm pretty sure is toxic but will probably result in me getting the clearer skin and "shiny" hair all the Blues girls have. What do you know?, I tell myself. It costs a lot of money to look this cheap. At night, I'm still on shadow-duty at the Blue Room. Perfect for me to figure out how the girls are chosen, how the best girls attract their clients. Which one might be my mysterious patron.

I wonder why no other patron's been chosen for me. After all, I've been here five days, with my so-called virtue still intact – in name, anyway. Has Terrence said something? Are they holding me for that patron? And if so – what are they waiting for? I'd told Terrence – I was ready, willing, and able to do whatever I had to do. I wasn't scared.

After four days of this, I'm going stir-crazy. I

almost wish for a client just to make the loneliness die down a bit. With no internet, there's just the hotel's mediocre list of new-releases to choose from, and I've already burned through all the sequels and action-films on offer. All that's left on my TV on-demand is the porn, and I get enough of that already.

I decide to head to the cafeteria.

Not that it stocks much, of course. It's where we can all go to get gluten-free snacks, bits of lettuce, and special green tea. I figure it's time to meet some of the other Blues girls.

They're all sitting together, and immediately I feel like it's middle school all over again. I'm the new girl in the lunchroom, and everyone's already goth their cliques down-pat. There's three of them – all a little older than I am – one with jet-black hair and a nose-ring, one nearly makeupless girl with long natural red hair, and one Miss-America-looking brunette who looks like she's just missing a tiara.

"So," whispers the Goth to the redhead, "what's all the fuss about?"

"I mean, she's pretty," Miss America says, "but I don't get why they're all requesting her."

The Blue Room (The Blue Room Vol. 1)

All requesting her? But nobody's been assigned to me yet...

"Maybe she can suck dick almost as good as Brandi here," the redhead points to the Goth.

"Maybe she's a really cunning linguist," Brandi grins. "Like you, Scarlett. We know how good your French and Russian are."

"She knows how to say *prick* in fifteen different languages," says the redhead.

Miss America raises her eyebrows. "Maybe she's a naughty school-teacher, like Julie. Giving *discipline*."

"Whatever she's got," says Brandi, "Terrence Blue wants some of her. You know how rarely he visits the Towers."

"Don't be jealous," Julie slaps her wrist lightly. "You know *you'd* blow Terrence Blue if you had the chance. And he wouldn't have to pay for it either."

"Let's just call it a buy-back," Scarlett giggles.

Then another girl walks in. Long, shiny dark hair. A self-assured walk. Dark olive skin.

"Rita?"

Against myself I whisper the name.

But the girl who turns to me in surprise isn't

Rita. Her smile, though, reminds me of Rita's. So kind. So sweet.

"Sorry..." I say. "I thought you were someone else."

"No problem," she says. "I'm sorry – I don't think we've met. I'm Roseanne." She laughs. "Not Roseanne. Roz. I changed my name when I came in here. I think it sounds more..."

"Slutty?"

We both giggle.

"Staci," I say.

"Oh, *you*'re Staci." Her mouth drops open.

"Why, what have you heard?"

"Nothing," her voice is sweet, almost shy. "Only that –,"

"What?"

"I know Terrence likes you a lot," she says.

My ears turn crimson. Does *everyone* at the Blue Towers know about my little liaison with Terrence Blue? For all the talk of discretion and privacy, it sure feel like the girls here haven't got any.

"Congratulations," she says.

"On what?" *Landing Terrence?* The idea feels

The Blue Room (The Blue Room Vol. 1)

almost distasteful when I say it out loud.

"You know what it means, don't you?" Her voice is low – like she doesn't want the other girls to hear.

"No, what?"

"He's saving you for someone really special. All the patrons have been asking for the new girl, and he's been stonewalling them all. Whatever he wants you to do – it's out of the ordinary. He only gets involved with the very best girls. The one he has plans for."

I think of the patron – my mysterious admirer – and grimace. I wonder what plans he and Terrence have for me, in the end.

"I don't know anything about any plans," I say.

She raises a dark, arched, eyebrow. "Well, all I know is – you're set up good." Her smile turns wry. "It's not all sordid here, you know. Some of us – we do more than play the part. We make it real."

"What do you mean?"

"I mean we fall in love." She looks almost blissful as she speaks. "We're brought into contact with some of the most handsome, most powerful, most desirable men in the world. And sometimes it's about more than the money. More than the sex. Sometimes, some of us lose ourselves in the fantasy. We fall in real, honest, love."

"I always thought that was a myth." *The prostitute with the heart of gold. Pretty woman.* All fantasy. All illusion.

"Nuh, uh," she shakes her head. "Not all of us end up bad. Some of us get married – or at least, become long-term mistresses. Some of us get the money to start our own businesses, to pursue our dreams..."

"To go to med school?"

I decide to see how much she knows.

As I expect, her smile vanishes.

"When I came in..." She's putting it all together. "You called me..."

I nod, slowly.

"You want to know what happened to..."

Again, I nod.

The girls at the other table are leaning in – trying to pretend like they're just stretching. They don't fool me. The walls have ears, here. Nowhere is really private.

"I'll tell you more tonight," she says. "Come to my room. It's number 231. I'm down the hallway from you. After eight."

The Blue Room (The Blue Room Vol. 1)

I can hardly contain my excitement. For the first time since I've gotten to the Blue Room, I've got something close to a lead. Roz knows who Rita is. She knows what might have happened to her. She knows *something*.

Alone, in my room, I watch the hours tick by until 8 pm. I'm antsy – fidgety. I can' t focus. I don't feel like a sexy glamorous femme fatale at all – just a bored kid who can't sit still. My thoughts about Terrence, my desire, everything – goes out the window. I'm focused on Rita, and that's all. I'm focused on finding the truth about what happened to her. And I'm close. I'm so close I can taste it.

I watch the clock tick by. **7:40. 7:45. 7:50.** The wait is excruciating, but I comfort myself with the thought that my search for answers might finally, finally, be at an end. This much, at least, I can look forward to.

At 8 pm I slip out of my room and tiptoe down the hall, trying not to attract too much attention. Already I know the others, girls like Scarlett and Brandi and Julie, are onto me. The last thing I want to do is give them more scope for gossip.

Roz's door is slightly ajar. She's left it open for me.

I don't bother knocking. I don't want to attract any attention. I just push it gently open and slip in.

And then I see her. Completely naked, her back facing me, her long lustrous hair tumbling almost to the sheets. Her back, arched. She's moaning.

She's sitting on the side of the bed, her legs stretched open wide; I can see the ecstasy shuddering through her. I can see him only in shadow – the man she's with – on his knees before her, his head between her legs.

He's going down on her. I flush in embarrassment, but my redness has another cause, too. I'm aroused – without knowing why – by the sight of it: by Roz screaming in ecstasy, by the man's tongue probing between her legs.

A surprise client? It shouldn't surprise me. Last-minute changes seem *de riguer* here in the Blue Room.

I know I should leave. I know I should get out. But I'm frozen to the spot, watching the two of them, watching how much Roz is enjoying herself.

Could I do this? I wonder. *Could I enjoy it*? My

whole body is tingling with excitement just thinking about it. For the first time, my body is so on fire I can't stand it. This isn't just desire. This is passion: overwhelming, overflowing.

Now Roz is raising him up; they're kissing, devouring one another, while she slips her hand down to his waist and begins massaging his member.

The lights are off, and I still can't see his face. Just his body: young, taut, handsome, as he thrusts into her, as she cries out.

"Oh, yes!" Her words run together. "Yes, yes! Oh – I love you – yes!"

It's just an act, I tell myself. She's saying what prostitutes are paid to say. But as she cries out "I love you" over and over, as she wraps her legs around his waist as he drives deeper into her, she seems totally genuine – totally enraptured. Totally in love.

I remember what Roz said earlier. Some girls fall in love. She'd looked so happy, then. Her cheeks had been pink, flushed.

Yes, I decide. Roz really is in love.

The man thrusts into Roz one final time and they come together, as one, shuddering with joy.

Kailin Gow

At last I am able to tear myself away from the sight. I run down the hall and reach my room. I've never been this aroused before. I can't stand it.

Against myself, my fingers search for my phone, scroll through for Terrence Blue's number, text him the words that have been floating around in my head all day.

Come over, now. I want you.

Chapter 12

*D*emanding, aren't we?

I blush when he answers me seconds after I text him.

What can I say? I write back. *I'm feeling...*

Bored? Lonely? Turned on? All three. I delete the words.

I'm in the mood for some fun, I write.

Terrence arrives within fifteen minutes.

Immediately we are in one another's arms, kissing passionately, devouring one another like there's no tomorrow. Images of Roz and her mysterious patron flash through my mind: of the arch of her back, of how her long hair tumbled down, of how she screamed with the patron's tongue darting between that cleft between her legs. I want Terrence to do all of that to me. I want it now.

Terrence seems to know what I want before I ask

for it. Without words he's tearing off my panties, throwing them across the room, stretching my legs wide with his palms before pressing his lips against me, his tongue playful, teasing – bringing me so close to pleasure, then letting me come down, so that I can never approach orgasm. The feeling is exhausting, tantalizing. I want it to go on forever. My desire to come mingles with the desire to make it last all night.

At last he uses his fingers, too, and then I'm over the edge. I come, so loudly that Terrence laughs softly, his chuckle deep in his throat.

"And to think," he murmurs. "When I met you, you were so...inexperienced. And now you're telling *me* to come over."

He traces my cheek with his fingertips, grinning. "Maybe *you're* the client?" he raises an eyebrow.

"And you're the whore?"

His smile darkens.

"I don't like that word," he said. "Not for you. Not for any of the girls."

"What are we, then?"

"Escorts? Professional mistresses? Courtesans? Call girls?"

The Blue Room (The Blue Room Vol. 1)

"Does it change anything? Except the price?"

Terrence looks grave. "It's more than a brothel I'm running here," he says. "It's a fantasy. For men and women alike. A chance for rich men and beautiful women to – mutually – make *both* their dreams come true."

"Is that what you're doing?" I ask him. "Making all *my* dreams come true?"

"I certainly hope so."

As he speaks, I feel almost ill. Part of me wants to call the whole thing off – to run away – to go back home to Vegas. I'm not interested in *fantasy*. I'm not interested in dreams coming true. Right now, I realize with a sickening jolt, I'm interested in a beautiful, unattainable boy with bright blue eyes and a wicked smile, who drives me wild, who I'm starting to have feelings for. The kind of feelings I can't trust. The kind of feelings that will make it really hard for me to sleep with just another patron.

Maybe Roz will have the answers, I think. *Roz will tell me what happened to Rita – and then I can leave...*

I don't want the money, anymore. I don't want

the designer clothes or the lessons in the contemporary global economy. I just want what Roz had with that man. Something like real, genuine love. Something I can hold onto.

"Staci?" Terrence is almost tender with me. "What is it?"

"What's going on, here?" My voice is low.

"What do you mean?"

"With us?"

His smile turns into a frown.

"What do you mean?"

"I mean – is this part of my *job*? Is this – training for my patron? Or is this something else?"

He is silent for a while.

"It was easier to think it was training you," he said. "It was easier to think – that this was just a sex thing. Or an almost-sex thing. I don't know. That's what I told myself when I cancelled your meeting with – well, with the client." He swallows. "But the truth is, I'm jealous. I'm not sure I want anyone else with you. I'm not sure I could stand to think about it."

"Can it be?" I try to sound smooth, but my voice is shaking. "Does the great Terrence Blue

The Blue Room (The Blue Room Vol. 1)

have...feelings?"

"Maybe." He shakes his head. "I mean – I don't do monogamy, Staci. I don't do relationships. With you, it started out as just attraction. But our chemistry is undeniable."

And it hits me.

I want him. I want to be with him. Maybe not forever – I'm smart enough to know he'll break my heart – but right now, he's all I want. More than the cash. More even than answers.

I don't want to sell my virginity for money. The sex I want is based in feelings, in emotions. Dare I say it – in love.

"I want you to take me," I say. "I want you to make love to me – right now."

He looks at me in surprise. "Are you sure?"

"If I'm *ruined* for your client, I don't care," I say. "I don't want my first sex to be for money. I don't want the money. Not yours, not anyone else's." I smile. "This one's on the house."

"Financially," he stammers. "I mean – as a businessman, I should tell you that this is a very stupid decision."

"And as a man?" I ask him.

His smile is sweet and sad. "As a man," he said, "nothing could make me happier than to be your first." He swallows. "If not your only."

"Do you have a condom?"

He nods. He reaches in his pocket.

And then we hear the shot.

One big boom. The shattering of windows.

I recognize the direction of the sound.

"Roz..." I whisper.

We rush to room 238, but we're too late.

In Roz's hand is a gun. And in Roz's forehead is a hole, gaping, bleeding, the blood trickling down into her glassy, open eyes.

Too many thoughts rush through me all at once. Panic. Terror. Fear. And rage – bitter, wild rage. I'm not seeing Roz's face there, there half-smashed with a bullet through the brain, but Rita's – the face of the girl I knew, the girl I loved, the girl whom I might have found, whom I'd *almost* found, and who was forever gone.

What if I hadn't texted Terrence? What if I'd waited outside her door for the client to leave?

The Blue Room (The Blue Room Vol. 1)

Would Roz still be alive? Would she have told me the truth of what happened to Rita?

I'm screaming, screaming my head off, barely aware of what I'm doing or why; I rush to her and then my hands are covered in her blood, Roz's blood, and still I'm thinking that it's Rita's.

Rita…what's become of Rita? Did she meet the same fate as Roz?

*****

This is the End of Part I

Thank you for reading The Blue Room Vol. *1.* **This is a multiple novella romance series. Part two and three will be available for pre-order soon.**

To be notified as soon as the next parts are released, please join the Kailin Gow Mailing List at
http://www.kailingow.com

Kailin Gow

Also, please feel free to like my Facebook page for more updates.

The Blue Room (The Blue Room Vol. 1)

GET INVOLVED!!!

If you enjoyed this novella, please leave a review, and recommend it to a friend.

*****

Let her know by leaving stars and letting her know what you like about
The Blue Room

*****

The Blue Room Series also features some characters from *The Never Knights Trilogy*

For 17 and Up

A quick read, all three books in The Never Knights Trilogy is available here:

Kailin Gow

The Blue Room (The Blue Room Vol. 1)

If you liked *The Blue Room*, you would like

Barely Legal

A New Adult Romantic Thriller

For Laura Turner, helping others had been her way of coping and forgetting a past so painful, she had to hide it from the ones she loved or risk going insane. Helping her best friend Serena Singleton start a new life free from a dark past, made her feel she was helping herself move forward.

Laura, whose family ran in the same circle as billionaire composer Sebastian Sorensen and lived a life many would envy, had secrets of her own, and it had been years since she'd lived free of the same addiction that consumed her friend Serena.

Kailin Gow

When Laura moved to Los Angeles to work at a law firm who hired her to start even without her passing the bar, she meets the mysterious and sexy Peter Townshend, whose irresistible charm and take charge personality brings out a part of her she had hidden for years.

Hidden behind a wall of secrets and giving her his orders, she only has his seductive voice to guide her to do his bidding. He knows all her buttons. He knows all about her.

He knows she's been a bad girl.

He knows good girls do bad things sometimes...even things that are...

Barely Legal

DON'T MISS IT!
Get Barely Legal here:

The Blue Room (The Blue Room Vol. 1)

http://www.amazon.com/Barely-Legal-Kailin-Gow/dp/1597480983